Serena quickly discovers that inheriting a cottage in the English Lake District is just the beginning of an adventure that leads her right into Paul Benson's arms.

Paul, a naturalistic painter, finds himself accompanying Serina into a dangerous situation in pursuit of picture thieves. The trail leads to Venice but back in the Lake District Serina is in peril from one of the gang. She is rescued by Paul at the last minute when he proposes marriage on a rickety bridge over a waterfall.

Love in the Lakes

ISBN: 978-1-4874-3810-4
Cover art by Angela Waters

Published by eXtasy Books Inc

Look for us online at:
www.eXtasybooks.com

Love In the Lakes

By

Pippa Newnton

Dedication

To Paul from Pippa.
Thank you for your help and encouragement.

Chapter One

I could feel Terry's hardness as he pressed against me. His hands caressed my body. In another moment I would have led him to my bed.

The door opened with a bang. It was Angela, my roommate.

"So that's where the two of you are." She flung her books down on her bed.

Terry moved away from me.

"It's all very well skipping a life class." Angela smiled. "From the look of it, you were about to have your own life class."

I could feel my cheeks going red. We were all at Brookshire Art College. Terry was my boyfriend, and until now the arrangement with Angela had worked well. I stayed out of her way when she was entertaining, and she stayed out of mine.

This afternoon was different. Terry had persuaded me to miss a class and we were about to have an afternoon in bed as Angela was safely in class until teatime, or so we thought.

She sat down on her own bed.

"I came back to tell you that the principal is looking for you."

"The Principal, what does he want?" I asked.

"No idea. He looked pretty serious. He wants you to go to his office."

Now what have I done? Has he found out that Terry and I have been cutting classes to have sex? Who would have told him? Not Angela.

"I suppose I'd better go and see what he wants." I shot Terry a look.

We went out of my room leaving Angela stretching out on her bed.

"What can this be about?" I asked Terry as we walked along the corridor.

He squeezed my hand. "It can't be anything serious. Probably just wants a chat about your grades. They've been pretty good so far, haven't they?"

I squeezed his hand back as we reached the door to the Principal's office.

"See you." He swung away down the corridor as I knocked lightly on the door.

"Come in," a voice called.

As I walked into Dr Peters' oak panelled room, he got up from behind his large mahogany desk looking serious.

I wondered what on earth was wrong. What was this all about?

He looked so stern, it was obviously something pretty important.

"Ah, Miss Spelton. Please sit down, Serina."

I sat in the chair facing him as he remained standing.

"I'm sorry to tell you," he said. "I have just received a telephone call to say that your parents have been involved in a car crash."

I could feel my heart beating quickly. "Are they . . ." I began.

Dr Peters came round the desk and put his hand on my shoulder.

"Your mother died instantly, but your father survived."

I stared at him not taking in what he had said, then tears came to my eyes. I must have fainted, for the next thing I knew I was sprawled in a chair and the College nurse was standing over me.

"I'm all right," I muttered, getting up unsteadily. The nurse guided me to the door. Dr Peters looked on with concern.

"Shall I come with you to your room?" the nurse asked.

"I will be fine," I shook off her hand and walked unsteadily into the corridor. When I reached my room, Angela had gone. I collapsed onto the bed and lay there for a long time.

The rest of the day was a nightmare. I remember saying goodbye to Angela. Terry saw me to the train station, but beyond that everything was a blur.

I arrived in Ormskirk, took a taxi to No. 2, Sinden Gardens. The front door was open, unusual in these times. As I walked into the front hall. I was met by our neighbour, Mrs Benson.

"He's in the bedroom, my dear. Best prepare yourself for a shock. Doctor has just left him. He looks frail, and I'm so sorry about your mother."

Mrs Benson was a good soul, but just at that moment all I wanted to do was rush upstairs to my father.

I stumbled up the stairs. His bedroom door was open. I hardly recognised the pale, wan figure in the bed.

He stretched out his hands to me as I entered the room.

It was a familiar room. The wallpaper I had helped put up years ago, now looking worse for wear, the text above the bed, *Peace in this house,* my mother's nightgown still on the chair beside the bed. Tears came to my eyes.

"Dad," I cried, rushing towards him. I held his hand, so frail, so fragile. There was nothing I could say. I felt his grip tighten, then he lay back on the pillows exhausted.

The days that followed were like a dream. I dealt with my mother's funeral, for which I needed to do everything for my father. There was no way I could go back to my art course. I stayed at home to look after him, my ambition to become an artist fading into the distance.

My father seemed to have given up on life and lay all day huddled up in a chair, head down. I looked after him as best I could, but one morning three years later, while taking him a cup of tea in bed, I found him apparently asleep and couldn't wake him. I sent for the doctor. When he came, he shook his head and gave me the bad news.

It rained at my father's funeral. Under dripping umbrellas, mourners moved slowly beneath the elm trees to the grave. It was like a dream, or nightmare. I know that we went back to the house for a funeral tea, but it seemed unreal, the rain continuing to pour down relentlessly. Everyone was very kind and wished me luck as they left until only my friends, Angela and Terry, remained. They came specially to be with me and I much appreciated their coming. They had both finished their courses and were now out in the world earning their living.

"Take it easy love." Angela guided me gently to the settee and sat me down.

Terry was standing awkwardly by the fireplace.

Angela sat beside me. "It's been a hectic, emotional day for you."

I felt tears coming to my eyes. "I've lost three years of my life while you two have graduated. My ambition to be an artist was put on hold while my father gradually faded away. I loved him dearly. I couldn't bear to see him suffer. There was no-one else to care for him." I sobbed into my handkerchief.

Terry came forward and held my hand. "You must feel as though the bottom has dropped out of your life, but you have your future before you. All that work at art school. You must take up the threads of where you left off."

I gave them both a hug. "Thanks for coming, I'm fine, it's just, you know . . ."

"I know, but I must go," Angela said. "I'm settled now in

London. As soon as I get back, I'll write and give you my address. I'm about to move into a new flat. Will you be all right?"

"Don't worry about me." I clutched my sodden handkerchief.

Terry obviously wanted to stay. He probably had sex in mind, but any feelings of that kind were long gone.

"Sorry Terry," I said, as he tried to kiss me. "Now is not the time, and perhaps it's never."

He pulled away looking disappointed. "I'm off to Europe next week on a painting tour but keep in touch, your feelings may change. I'll have my iPad with me. Here's my email address." He took an old envelope from his pocket and wrote the address down. He gave me a tiny kiss and was gone.

Left alone, I walked through the empty rooms of the house, which echoed their sadness back to me.

I lay in bed that night, my thoughts in turmoil. What should I do? Who could I turn to? I thought of my Aunt Em living in the Lake District. She was now my only living relative. Should I go to her and ask for advice? I was usually so sure of myself, but now my world seemed to have turned upside down.

Thoughts tumbled through my head but I must have fallen asleep, as then it was morning.

At first I didn't want to get out of bed to face the world, but I plucked up courage. Swinging my feet into slippers, I padded across to the window. The house was in the middle of a terrace of houses all depressingly the same except for little touches like the window box of pansies put on the downstairs windowsill, long since faded away. Looking out I could see people walking to work, some hastening without purpose, some off to jobs, going shopping, taking children to school. The day was bright with sunshine but a black cloud hovered over me. What was my purpose in life? I washed and dressed, then went downstairs to prepare breakfast.

As I boiled the kettle I suddenly realised that I was free, free to become a painter again. A wave of relief swept over me. I knew what I would do. I would go to see Aunt Em, stay awhile, and do some painting in the Lake District.

I looked up her phone number in my diary, took my mobile phone, and dialled the number.

The phone rang and rang but no-one answered. Perhaps she was out shopping.

I looked at my watch. It wasn't even nine o'clock. Surely she wouldn't be out this early?

Anyway, I would stick to my plan. I was excited. My chance to become a painter at last!

I went back to my breakfast and as I did so, the doorbell rang. It was the postman. Registered delivery. He handed me an unusual envelope. It gave the impression that it contained a legal document. My hand shook as I opened it. It was from a solicitor's office in Ambleside in the Lake District.

The letter was direct and abrupt.

"We are sorry to inform you that your aunt Miss Emily Renault has died and you are the sole benefactor under her will."

I sat down heavily on the settee with a cup in my hand, breakfast forgotten, staring into space. I looked at the cup. It was decorated with apples and plums.

I remembered this cup. It had been a wedding present to my parents long before I was born. On one occasion as a child, I broke a saucer and cried bitterly until my mother soothed me, saying that it was easy to get a replacement. Tears came to my eyes.

Not so easy to replace parents or Aunt Em. Once they were gone, they were gone. Now I was alone in the world. I wandered upstairs and into my father's room. So many memories, his hairbrush still with grey hair clinging to it, Mother's photograph on the bedside table.

I sat down with a bump in his old armchair next to the bed. Memories came flooding back. My happiest memory was when I was seven. We were in the Lake District with Aunt Em, taking a picnic in the hills. I played roly-poly down the slope with my father catching me at the bottom. I could still taste the picnic, the tomatoes in the salad, cracking the shells of the hard-boiled eggs and peeling them, the crisp lettuce, even the bread seemed special. Happy times, but now all gone.

This won't do, pull yourself together. I'm twenty five years old, slim, blue eyed, auburn hair, not beautiful, a bit dowdy in my old sweater and jeans but presentable. With or without parents and Aunt Em, I've a lifetime in front of me.

I went downstairs and picked up the letter again. It invited me to go to Ambleside in the Lake District to discuss the will. I would go.

Chapter Two

The solicitors in Ambleside were called Preston and Plant. I rang them up, and a very pleasant voice commiserated me on my loss and suggested that I should stay at the Lakeside Hotel in Ambleside and go to see them soon after I arrived.

Ormskirk to Ambleside was not the easiest journey, and in addition to my two suitcases, I took a pack of sandwiches and a book to read on the train. It took over two hours and involved two changes of train. The 10.41 am from Ormskirk, change at Preston and then Oxenholme, reaching Windemere at 12.44 pm.

On the way I ate my sandwiches, bought a coffee from the restaurant car buffet, and read my book, which was what father used to call a penny dreadful, a paperback novel about love amid the coal mines of the north, but it passed the time pleasantly enough.

Arriving at Windermere I took a taxi, which wound along the lakeside road to Troutbeck, where Beatrix Potter used to live. *I must visit the museum sometime.*

The taxi didn't go through the village, as the modern road goes over Troutbeck Bridge and then on into Ambleside.

Arriving at Ambleside, we drew up outside the Lakeside Hotel, an impressive white building. The driver took my cases into the hotel. I was greeted by a fresh-faced receptionist introducing herself as Sally Chivers.

She called a porter to show me to my room.

The porter was a small lad who, after taking me to the room

and putting my cases down near the wardrobe refused the tip I tried to press on him.

"All part of the service," he said, handing me the room key.

I sat on the bed and looked around. The room was pleasant and airy. I went to the window. There was a view over the lake. I opened the window and leant out, breathing in the fresh pure air. So different from the air in Ormskirk, always tainted by factory smoke.

After unpacking, I spent what was left of the afternoon exploring the town. I walked past Preston and Plant's office in the High Street, resisting the temptation to pop in and say hello. Time enough for that tomorrow.

I walked down to the lakeside. The water was calm, yachts wheeled like seagulls, white sails flapping in the breeze. I watched the ferry offloading its passengers, who crowded onto the pier, women with children, men in business suits fresh from the office, tourists looking round in wonder.

That evening I went into the sumptuous dining room of the hotel, so large that the scattering of guests seemed dwarfed by their surroundings. After an excellent meal I sat in the lounge with coffee. My book was with me as I intended to read for a while but I began to feel sleepy and so went up to my room, tumbling into the soft and welcoming sheets.

I slept well, and the next day went down to breakfast. Voices in the dining room were muted, as though those present were still half asleep. After a good breakfast I went in search of the solicitor's office. As I went out onto the street, the sun came out from behind a cloud, a good omen perhaps? I walked down the High Street. Preston and Plant's office, sandwiched between a gift shop and a laundrette, came into view. As I went in, I was greeted by a short, tubby, red-faced gentleman dressed formally in a black suit, white shirt and black tie.

"Come in, come in. You must be Miss Spelton?"

"How did you know?" I asked.

"There's a strong likeness to your aunt. Yes indeed. I'm Mr Preston, sit yourself down and we will give you all the details."

Mr Preston was so like Mr Pickwick, the character created by Charles Dickens, that instead of telling me about Aunt Em, I felt that he should be setting off on his travels. However, he took some papers off his desk and after coughing politely, read out the details.

The particulars of Aunt Em's will were simple and direct. I was the only beneficiary, so the house and its contents were mine.

"Regrettably," said Mr Preston, "there isn't a great deal of money involved, as your Aunt was not a rich woman, but it is yours, such as it is."

He put several documents in front of me.

I should have read them, but I decided to trust him and signed them.

He gave me a keyring, the keys on it jangling as he handed them to me.

"The house is a few miles from here, but there is a small community, the village of Little Tenderden, and your nearest neighbour has agreed to look after the house until you arrive. When would you like to go to see it?"

"Tomorrow, I think." I decided that morning to stay another night in the hotel to have more time to explore the town. I would then set off on my adventure.

We shook hands, and I said goodbye and walked back out onto the street feeling a sense of excitement. I went back to the hotel.

Sally was still on the reception desk. Fortunately my room was free for the extra night and Sally told me that the village, Little Tenderden, was about ten miles outside Ambleside. She said that there was an excellent taxi service in the town, mentioning Sid Chapman as a reliable driver. From the way she spoke about him I thought there was some sort of romantic attachment. Sally agreed to book him for ten o'clock the next day.

I spent the rest of the day mingling with the crowds of tourists, ate tea in a rather nice old-fashioned cafe, then went back to my room, read my book and snoozed until dinnertime.

Next morning, Sid Chapman turned up at ten o'clock sharp wearing a peaked cap and a cheeky grin. I was waiting in the lobby with my suitcases as he came in, and I could tell from the way he greeted Sally that I was right about the romantic attachment.

It was a lovely day. There's something about the English Lake District. Maybe it's the air, the feeling of open space, the hills and trees, the water. I could feel the stress going out of my body. There was a delicious feeling of adventure and not knowing what was to come next.

The taxi wound along the meandering roads and up into the hills past the Skelton Bridge Hotel, where it took a right turn past a small General Store and a cluster of houses, up a narrow track, and then we reached the house.

"There it is," Sid said, pointing. Surrounded by a copse of trees was a weather-beaten stone cottage not at all as I remembered it. It seemed much smaller than when I'd visited as a child, but there were roses round the porch and the sun shone down on them, inviting me to come to what was to be my new home.

Sid took my cases and deposited them on the doorstep. As I turned to pay him, the front door opened and a young girl stood framed in the opening.

"Hi, Nancy." Sid seemed to know everyone.

"Hi Sid," she said, then turning to me. "You must be Miss

Spelton. I'm Nancy Barker. My mum Sonia is in the kitchen, we've been waiting for you."

Sid waved goodbye as Nancy helped me with my cases.

Sonia Barker came out of the kitchen wiping the flour from her hands on a cloth.

"I was just making a pie for your supper," she said. "We thought you wouldn't have time to go out to get anything, so we have left a few things for you."

I could tell that Sonia loved to talk as she immediately launched into an account of the neighbourhood.

"We live just down the road at the farm. There are four cottages down there. Jed Thompson and his wife Marion live in one. They don't have any children and Jed is a bad lot by all accounts. Teddy Barnes lives in one of the other cottages. He used to come up and do a bit of gardening for Miss Renault. Then there's a mystery man, at least that's what Nancy calls him. Moved into the district recently but keeps very much to himself. Old Rosy Profit lives in the end cottage. She's a nice old girl but is inclined to be sharpish sometimes. I expect you will meet them all in due course."

I felt a bit overwhelmed by this sudden burst of information.

Sonia looked fondly at her daughter. "A great friend of Miss Renault was Nancy. She used to help her with the housework. Would you like Nancy to come up and help you, Miss Spelton?"

"That would be very kind of you. I would appreciate some help at least until I get sorted out."

"I'd be pleased to do it," Nancy said. "Miss Renault was a nice old lady, but she got to be ailing and when she went to hospital she never came out." She turned, her eyes full of tears.

"We were devastated when she died. When the solicitors told us that you would be coming, we felt we ought to tidy the place up a bit for you, although we thought you would be a bit older." Sonia wiped her hands on her apron in embarrassment. "Is there anything else we can do for you?"

"No, thank you, all I want to do now is settle in and have a bit of a rest."

"Of course you do, my dear. Nancy will show you the bedrooms. We've cleaned them up, aired the beds and changed the sheets and pillowcases, so you will be all snug tonight."

It was very kind of them, but after a long train journey the day before, the excitement of the day, the taxi ride and all the local information, I felt my energy was totally drained.

Nancy took me up to the main bedroom. It was like stepping back in time. Everything was like a time warp. There were dolls sitting on the cupboard at the side of the bed, and by the window were two ragged teddy bears.

Nancy then showed me into the second smaller bedroom across the landing.

The wallpaper was an awful brown colour. The room was sparsely furnished with just a single bed and in one corner a small door. I went over to it and tried the handle. It was locked.

"Does this lead to the attic?" I asked.

"I don't know," Nancy replied. "I'll ask Mum if she knows where the key is."

"Don't bother now," I said. "You go down. I'll come down in a minute."

As Nancy left, I went back into the main bedroom and sank down wearily onto the bed.

After a while I felt better and spent a little time unpacking and opening drawers. One of them stuck slightly but I jammed it back hard.

I went downstairs into the sitting room. There was an old

piano with a fretted front, two comfortable but sagging armchairs in front of an art deco fireplace that would fetch a fortune at auction. The effect was one of comfort, like an old shoe fitting its owner exactly.

I could hear Sonia and Nancy moving about in the kitchen, so I went to talk to them.

Sonia was just closing the door on an Aga cooker. "There's a local shop and post office just down the road and a supermarket in Ambleside, but you will be all right until tomorrow. There's fresh eggs, cheese, milk and bread for your breakfast and the pie will be done in about an hour. Don't forget to take it out. I'll send Nancy up in the morning to see if you are all right. Come on Nancy, we must get back."

She clapped her hat on her head and they were off, leaving me alone in a strange house.

Chapter Three

A house can be mournful and depressing but I felt comfortable in this loved and cared for house. It did seem smaller than when I visited as a child, but still felt like home.

Now I was on my own, I felt at a loose end. Wandering aimlessly for a while, I decided to take a look at the garden. The sun was going down, but there was still enough light to see by. A cloud of rooks wheeled overhead, settling down in the trees beyond the garden. The garden itself showed evidence of neglect. There were formal flower beds now speckled with weeds, but there was still a riot of colour, dahlias, begonias, and a white flower that I couldn't identify but which shone out luminously in the half light. I turned and went back into the house. Time to explore properly tomorrow.

Turning on the lights, I was reminded of the pie by the delicious smell coming from the kitchen. I went in and with a cloth took it out of the oven. It was done to perfection. I set it aside to cool a little before cutting into it.

It took me a while to find plates and cutlery, but eventually I managed.

The pie was delicious. Mrs Barker was a good cook. She had left me a bowl of fruit, so I took a peach, biting into it, releasing its delicate flavour. Afterwards I settled down to read one of my blood and thunder books. I must confess to being a fan of the sort of romantic fiction where the hero, a tall broad shouldered, blond giant is standing bare chested chopping wood while the heroine, a liberated female stands admiringly before him, then leaps onto a horse and gallops with him into the sunset sort of thing.

I found myself yawning, and the book slipped from my fingers. I picked it up and realised that I must lock up. This was always my routine when in Ormskirk.

After I'd staggered round the house locking the doors and putting the lights out, I went to bed, snuggling down into the crisp sweet smelling sheets.

I woke to sunlight pouring through the curtains. Slippers on, I padded to the window, patted the teddy bears on the head, drew the curtains back and looked down, not on a street of people in a town but on a vista of greenery, mountains in the distance beyond the trees echoing the blue of the sky with the grey of the fluffy clouds above.

I stretched, yawned, and went down to make my breakfast.

Everything I needed was there, thanks to Sonia. Deciding to have a boiled egg, I realised that I didn't know how to work the Aga. Mercifully it was still hot and I was able to boil water on it, but I knew that eventually I would have to learn to add fuel and riddle out the ashes—but not at this moment. Good butter on thick slices of toast with the egg and some tea. A satisfying breakfast.

Now how to begin the day? I needed to decide whether I was going to stay or to sell the house. I took out my notebook, turned to a fresh page and wrote at the top *Go* and *Stay*. Someone knocked at the front door. It was Nancy. I unlocked the door and let her in.

"You lock your door," she said in surprise. "We never lock ours."

"It's a city habit. Perhaps you don't need to in the country."

She smiled and nodded. "I've brought you some fresh

milk. Mum said I was to take you to the local shop and introduce you when you're ready."

"I am ready now." I closed the notebook.

Nancy was amused when I locked the front door as we went out.

"It's such a habit," I explained. "Maybe I shall get used to leaving it open soon."

The village shop was only a short walk, set in the cluster of cottages.

Nancy introduced me to Mrs Lisabet Clindly, a large motherly woman who shook my hand and welcomed me. The shop was quite small but crammed with goods. The aroma of cheese, ham and coffee filled the air, the brightly coloured packs crowding in upon each other.

With Lisabet and Nancy's help I managed to put together everything I was likely to need.

Nancy helped me carry them back to the cottage. "Mrs Clindly has most things in her shop, but as Mum said, the supermarket in Ambleside has a larger range of things."

"Thanks Nancy, I have to go to Ambleside soon to buy some painting materials."

Nancy looked at me in wonder. "Are you a painter then?" she asked.

"I want to be. I went to art school but haven't had much time to paint until now." As I said it, I realised that there was no need to write down the *for and against* list. My subconscious made up its mind for me. I was going to stay and paint in the Lake District. The cottage and the landscape already claimed me. As I stood in the doorway to say goodbye to Nancy I looked out across the trees to the mountains beyond, shrouded in a light mist, the sun was warming the straggling tentacles and dispersing them into the sky. Turning back into the house, I found my *for and against* list and tore it up.

For the rest of the day I laid my plans. I would paint the beauty spots of the area. I made a list of the materials I would need, paints, brushes, a pallet, turpentine to clean the brushes, an easel, and some canvases together with a notepad and crayons for preliminary sketches.

Then, for a change I went into the garden for a breath of fresh air. I stopped at a statue of a maiden holding a stone trough. Was this a fountain or just an ornament?

As I stood contemplating it, an old man with long, straggly hair, dressed in a ragged coat and trousers, came up the weed strewn path.

"What do you want?" I stepped back, startled.

"I don't mean no harm," he said. "That there's a fountain, but the waterpipe's broken. I'm Ted, Teddy Barnes. I lives in one of the farm cottages down there. I used to tidy the garden up a bit afore Miss Emily passed away, and I thought perhaps you would like to take me on?"

Judging by the state of the garden, tidying up must have happened some time ago, but I said, "Well, Ted, I do need someone to work on the garden, so I will give you a try. Do you have any tools?"

He pointed to a small tumbledown shed at the bottom of the garden. "They'm all in there." He touched his forelock. "Thank you, missy. I comes Tuesday and Thursday if that suits you?"

"Yes, that suits me very well," I said.

He shambled off and I went down to the shed and looked inside. There were all the usual forks, spades, hoes and rakes and I could see an old armchair with its stuffing coming out. Obviously Ted had made himself a little home there, but it was good that someone would do the heavy work in the garden so that I could enjoy the more exciting work of planting.

I wandered back up the garden and into the house. Then I realised that I hadn't asked him how much he charged. Oh well, it couldn't be much, otherwise Aunt Em wouldn't have employed him.

My next thought was, how do I get into Ambleside? I couldn't use taxis all the time. How about a bicycle? No, better a car. If I'm going to be going round the area painting, I need some form of reliable transport.

That settled, I made a cup of tea and munched a chocolate biscuit.

I spent the rest of the day pottering about, enjoying the freedom of doing absolutely nothing.

Next day I phoned for Sid's taxi to take me into Ambleside.

It was a glorious morning, and as the car arrived, a blackbird hopped across the lawn looking for worms. Last night's rooks set off from the trees in search of breakfast.

"I'm off to buy paints," I said to Sid as I sat beside him.

"I know a good painting and decorating shop," he said. "Shall I take you there?"

"No, Sid, I'm not painting the house, although I might want to do that later. No, I want to buy paints to paint pictures."

"I know just the place to take you. There's a lot of painters in Ambleside. They all get their supplies from Humbles in the High Street."

I sat back enjoying the ride as the car curved in and out of the winding roads down to town. Then I suddenly thought, Sid seemed to know everyone in the area, so why not ask him about a car.

"I don't suppose you know where I could buy a good second-hand car at a reasonable price, Sid? I'm going to need it to travel around on my painting trips, and I don't like the idea of carrying my stuff on a bicycle."

"Stod's Garage is what you want. Old Bert Stod is a friend of mine. He'll give you a good deal. Tell him I sent you. I'll drop you off there now. Afterwards you'll find Humbles Art Shop in the main street."

Stod's garage was a small place crammed between a dry cleaners and a convenience store in a side road next to the High Street. There was a tiny forecourt with four cars for sale. A stout man clad in a blue overall was standing looking at them.

As I got out of the taxi the man waved at Sid and he waved back.

"How can I help you?" the man asked, smiling at me.

"I want to buy a car," I said.

"Well you've come to the right place." He waved his hand around. "I'm Bert Stod and I'll bet young Sid said I would give you a fair price?"

"Yes, he did. I'm planning on doing some painting in the area, so I want a reasonable car to carry my things around in."

He looked thoughtful, then said, "I've got just the thing for you. It's out the back, come on through." He led me through the small showroom and into the yard at the back. Wiping his hands on an oily rag he pointed to an old Morris Minor sitting in a corner of the yard. "It's my favourite. None of this fancy modern stuff. I've been using it for a long time. Perfect running order. Maintain it myself. Used to belong to an old maiden lady. What do you think?"

I took one look at it, and I knew this was the car for me.

He opened the door and I sat in the driver's seat. Looking round I could see that the upholstery was in good condition.

"Can I take it for a test drive?"

"Of course you can. If you wait a moment I can put some trade plates on and we'll go for a spin."

I fell in love with the car straight away. It was just what I wanted. Bert asked for a reasonable price and things were soon fixed up.

"It's already licensed, so we just have to transfer ownership. How about insurance? Albernies in the High Street will fix you up with that. Take your documents along now." He handed them to me and wrote out a receipt for the money.

I went to Albernies, and the young man there was friendly and cheerful. I paid a cheque and was assured that I could now drive the car.

Before going back to the garage, I enquired the way to Humbles Art Shop. To my surprise it was close by. As I went into the shop, the doorbell jangled. There was the smell of paint in the air as I stepped over the threshold. I could see at a glance that it was very well equipped with everything I wanted and more.

An oldish man who turned out to be Mr Humble, the proprietor, came to serve me personally, helping me choose a range of pigments, canvases, a lightweight easel, sketch pad and crayons, together with turpentine and brushes. He, like everyone in Ambleside, was very helpful.

"We have a number of painters in this area as you can imagine. You must join our little gatherings at the Town Hall once a month. That's where we show our paintings, mainly for the tourists. I'll give you the name of the organiser and her phone number." He wrote it down for me.

I went back to the garage with Joe, Mr Humble's assistant, who carried my purchases for me and helped put them in the car while Bert Stod stood making encouraging noises. I showed him the insurance certificate, thanked him, then drove out of the yard and onto the road. The car was easy to drive and I soon felt confident with it. Bert had shown me a way to avoid the High Street so I made my way out of Ambleside the back way and soon was on the road to what I now felt was home.

After dinner, my thoughts turned to Angela and Terry, my friends from College. I didn't have Angela's address. She would have written to me in Ormskirk and whoever bought our house had probably thrown the letter away with all the junk mail that came through the door.

Terry's email address was somewhere around but when I came to look for the envelope he had written on I couldn't find it. Sadly I realised that the final links with my old life were completely severed. It was time to make a new life.

Chapter Four

Next morning I awoke to birdsong. It was a glorious morning and I felt like exploring. So after breakfast I changed into stout walking shoes. The sun was shining, but clouds were coming up over the horizon. Would it rain? I didn't think so, but I put my old mac on just in case.

I stood on the doorstep and breathed in the sweet-smelling air as Nancy came up the drive carrying the milk.

"Morning Nancy," I called.

"Sorry I'm a bit late Miss Spelton." She was out of breath. "There were some chores for Mum before I came this morning. Would you like me to help you with the housework?"

"No, not today but tell your mum the pie was delicious, thank you. Would you put the milk away for me? I'm going for a walk, it's such a lovely day."

"If you wait a minute, I'll walk you down to the farm. I can introduce you to my dad. He will be pleased to meet you."

"Thanks, I'd like to meet him. Go on in, You see I haven't locked the door."

Nancy smiled and went into the house while I waited on the doorstep.

When she came out we set off down the drive, the gravel crunching under our feet.

It felt good to be in the country, the birds singing, the air so fresh.

We arrived at the farm, a fine whitewashed building standing in a yard with chickens clucking, kittens running around, and a cockerel keeping an eye on everything.

"Dad's round the back feeding the pigs. Come on round." Nancy led the way.

I was glad to have stout shoes on, as the piggery wasn't exactly the place for dainty footwear. A rich fruity smell filled the air.

A figure in the distance straightened up as Nancy squelched towards him.

"Dad, I've brought Miss Spelton to say *hello*."

"Don't come any closer," he called, striding towards us. "It's not exactly the flavour of the month." He shook my hand. "I'm Fred Barker. Nice to meet you but Nancy shouldn't have brought you round the pigs."

"I don't mind." I looked at the stocky figure, his deep-set eyes twinkling. "I've met your wife, of course, and she and Nancy are looking after me."

"It's the least we can do. Good neighbours are important. If there is anything you ever need just let us know. I must go back." He turned and waved.

We retreated from the piggery.

"Thank you Nancy, it was good to meet your dad."

"Come in and say hello to Mum before you go."

"Just for a minute then, I'm supposed to be going for a walk."

"There's a good walk if you go down to the cottages, past the shop," she said. "Go round the trees in the dell and back again, there's an old slate quarry down there, but come and say *hello* to Mum first. "

Nancy took me into the farmhouse. We wiped our feet on the mat. The smell of fresh baked bread wafted out of the kitchen where Sonia stood preparing lunch.

"Stay awhile." She wiped her hands on her apron.

"I mustn't, I only came in to say *hello*. I met your husband at the pigs."

"Nancy, you never took Miss Spelton round to the pigs?"

"I wish you would both call me Serina," I said. "But now I really must be off."

As I made to go, Sonia called after me, "Come to tea soon we'll have freshly baked scones."

I walked down to the cottages and then I remembered that I needed some sugar and so went into the shop, its bell jangling.

Mrs Clindly was there talking to a man dressed in a short sleeved jacket and army style trousers.

He turned as I entered and said, "You must be Miss Spelton? Welcome to Tenderden." He was carrying a stout stick and his face was leathery and weather beaten. The skin around his eyes crinkled as he smiled.

"Does everyone know my name?"

Mrs Clindly smiled. "Not much you can keep secret if you live in a village like this, my dear."

"I'm Roy Blinks." He stretched out his hand.

I shook it. "Don't let me interrupt you, I've only come in for a bag of sugar."

"Ladies first. In any case I was only having a good chinwag."

I took my sugar, said goodbye and went out into the road. To my surprise, as I walked out I was confronted by a sullen-looking beast of a man.

He smelt, was unshaven, and was wearing a dirty torn jacket. "You'll be that woman up at the Renault place." He stared hard at me.

I stepped back in alarm. "What of it?"

"Miss Renault promised her cottage to me." He moved close to me. The smell was overpowering.

I was just about to run into the shop when the shop bell jangled and Roy Blinks came out.

"What's this about, Jed Thompson?" He waved his stick.

"Never you mind." The man rapidly turned and, to my surprise, hurried off.

I leant back on the door frame, my heart pounding.

"Nothing to worry about," said my new friend. "That was an undesirable neighbour, Jed Thompson. He lives in the cottage up the road."

"Thanks for rescuing me, Mr Blinks. That gave me quite a shock."

"Call me Roy. Jed Thompson is a thoroughly bad lot. We are unfortunate to have such a bad character living amongst us. If you ever get in trouble with him let me know. What did he say to you?"

"I don't know what he was talking about. He said my aunt promised my house to him. My aunt left the house to me in her will. I haven't heard anything about any other claim on it."

"I expect he was just trying it on. He's our local thief and liar. Forget about him. Were you going for a walk?"

"I was," I said, clutching the bag of sugar. "But now I think I ought to take this back home."

"Nonsense. Leave it with Lisabet in the shop, collect it on the way back. I can show you a good circular walk. I walk it every day for exercise."

"Thanks, I would like that. I'll just pop back into the shop."

Mrs Clindly took the sugar. "I'll keep it safe till you come back. Roy goes on his walk every day. He'll show you the way."

I thanked her, and we set off.

We went out of the village, up the hillside, and down to a copse of trees, the green hills rising all around us.

"I get a sense of freedom here, it reminds me of my childhood," I said, striding along beside him.

He was obviously an experienced walker judging by the

pace he set. He waved his stick. "You don't get anything like this in cities. Here we have fresh air, open spaces, and room to breathe."

We were now going through the trees, leaf mould softening our steps. We came to the slate quarry that Nancy mentioned. I could see that it was out of use. There was a mountain of broken slate piled up behind a low wire fence.

"Don't ever try to climb it," Roy said. "It's treacherous. I tried it once and nearly broke my ankle."

"Don't worry. I remember the time I twisted my ankle on a walk in these very hills."

We skirted round the base of the mound and out into open country again.

"You can go on if you wish." He waved his stick at the lake. "You can walk along the shoreline for quite a distance, or we can go back, which is what I normally do."

"I'll come back with you," I said.

We turned and followed the track past the slate quarry, through the trees, and back to the village shop, where I recovered my bag of sugar from Mrs Clindly.

Roy was waiting for me outside the shop as I came out.

"Thanks, Roy, I enjoyed that. Perhaps you will come to tea sometime soon?"

"I would like that." He waved goodbye with his stick.

I walked back to the house feeling good about new friends but then as I opened the front door I remembered Jed Thompson.

Would he ever follow up on his threat? Perhaps I should start locking the front door again, as he could walk in at any time.

Chapter Five

Time for my first excursion. I packed the car, putting my lunch in a backpack—cheese sandwiches, a flask of tea, and milk separately in a small bottle. From long experience I knew that tea doesn't taste the same if you put the milk in the flask, and I thought that cheese sandwiches would be safer than ham. As an indulgence I included a small bar of chocolate, although I felt a bit guilty that I hadn't included any fruit—perhaps next time!

For my equipment, I took only a sketchpad and a set of crayons and a ground sheet with me on this first trip.

I'd found a book of waterfalls in the Lake District on the shelf in my bedroom. The first one in the book was Stock Ghyll Force near Ambleside village so I decided to go there. I went to the car. The sun was out, the birds were singing, and I felt happy.

Parking the car in Ambleside, I took my backpack, pad and crayons and set out to walk to the Force. It was uphill, but the journey took me through Stock Ghyll Wood.

I walked through the canopy of trees, following a well-trodden path. The air was clean and sweet. I reached the top of the falls, remembering my painting tutor's advice not to choose a site too quickly but to explore all possible angles first.

I walked down to the foot of the falls, moss covered rocks, ferns, and leaf mould covering the way. The spray from the falls filled the air as I descended. The falls consisted of two streams rushing down and feeding into one foaming and bubbling torrent. The best view seemed to be from the bottom, so putting down my ground sheet, I sat on a lichen covered rock, settling down to make some preliminary sketches.

I wasn't alone, as quite a few people were walking along the beck, and some, less nervous than the rest, came up and looked over my shoulder at the sketch I was making. It was so long since I had done outdoor work that at first it was distracting, but then it was pleasant to exchange a word or two, and eventually I forgot the people and sank deeper into myself as I began to rough out the details.

Time passed quickly and I started to feel hungry. My flask and sandwiches were in the backpack. I got up, stretched and made my way across to a small clearing nearby where I found a bench seat overlooking the falls. As I opened my sandwiches, a small brown terrier bounded out of nowhere and sat at my feet. I was debating whether I should feed it when an old lady, carrying a walking stick, came up the path and sat beside me.

"Sorry about Jimpy. He's always looking for something to eat. Don't give him anything. Here, Jimpy." She held out a biscuit, which he jumped for, then settling down at our feet chewing happily.

"I'm Isobel Santir." She settled herself comfortably on the seat, and then added, "I was what we called an exotic dancer in my day." She laughed, waving her stick, "You wouldn't think it now, but I was famous. What do you do?" she asked abruptly.

I was taken aback by her direct approach, but then decided that she was probably used to getting her own way, hence her manner.

"I'm Serina Spelton, I have been looking after an invalid father for several years but now he has passed away, I hope to fulfil my ambition to become an artist."

That sounded a bit stuffy, but it was the truth. I thought she might ask what I was doing in the Lake District, but apparently what I said satisfied her.

"You must come and visit our little gatherings." She patted Jimpy who, having finished his biscuit, was looking for more. She went on, "Local artists show their paintings once a month in the Town Hall for the tourists, and then I hold a reception for the artists at my house in the evening." She searched in her handbag and drew out a card. "The next one is on Thursday at eight o'clock. Do come."

I put the card carefully in my backpack. "I would love to but I don't have any paintings yet." I felt a little overwhelmed by this formidable woman.

"Don't worry about that. Just come in the evening and meet everyone. I must go on with my walk—come on, Jimpy." She got up and put her dog on a lead. She went off, treading carefully to avoid the tree roots on the path, Jimpy trailing reluctantly behind her.

I looked in my backpack and found Mr Humble's note. As I expected, comparing it with Isobel Santir's card, the names and telephone numbers were the same. I decided that I would go to the gathering on Thursday, as it would be interesting to meet other artists from the area. I might pick up some tips.

Lunch finished, I went back to my perch by the waterfall.

The light began to fade as I completed my sketch, so I packed up and headed for home.

I drove up and parked the car as usual but when I got out I was surprised to see my two suitcases sitting on the front step.

I could hear someone moving about in the house. I went over and cautiously opened the front door. I remembered I hadn't locked it.

"Who's there?" I called out.

To my horror Jed Thompson appeared from the dining room holding a stick.

"What are you doing in my house?" I asked, retreating.

As before he was uncouth, wearing a ragged jacket and smelling of manure. He towered over me, and I thought he was going to strike me.

"Your house is it?" he rumbled, advancing. "I told you this house was promised to me. I'm clearing you out." He waved his stick.

I'm not exactly brave, but I stood my ground. "If you don't get out of my house, I'll call the police," I said.

He laughed. "Old Ralph Watkins won't help you much. He lives over the hill and has only got a bike. Still, I don't want any trouble, you will learn." Then, pushing me roughly aside he walked off down the path.

He turned and flung words back at me, "You'll rue the day you moved into this house."

I was shaking terribly, but as he disappeared from view, I managed to carry my suitcases back into the house. The smell of manure lingered in the air.

I thought I would find the house trashed, but to my surprise everything looked normal. Only my own personal things were moved out of the drawers and wardrobe. I was still shaking from the encounter. I thought a nice cup of tea might steady me, so I went into the kitchen, which as far as I could see, hadn't been touched, and made a cup of tea.

I sat for quite a while. Finally I began to recover and started thinking logically. I realised that I would have to change the locks on the doors and start to lock them again.

I felt the need to talk to someone, so I locked the door and went down to the farm to see Sonia.

I could hear the quaver in my voice as I told her about my encounter.

"Jed Thompson is a bad lot. He lives in the farm cottage

just down the lane. I wonder what gave him the idea of trying to claim your cottage."

"I've no idea. Not only did he try to turn me out of the house, but he threatened me as I was coming out of the shop yesterday. I was saved by Mr Blinks."

"Now that's an interesting one," Sonia leant towards me. "Mr Mystery, we call him. Seems to be a military man. He suddenly appeared and took old Mother Barnaby's cottage after she passed away and her son put it up for rent. Anyway, Jed's got a bad name in these parts. If there's anything bad going on in the neighbourhood, then he's bound to be in it." She pressed a batch of scones on me. "Just fresh from the oven."

I felt better from talking it out with her, so I thanked her and turned to go.

"Nancy will be up to see you tomorrow with the milk and to help you with the housework. Never mind Jed. If you get in any more trouble, my husband will see him off for you."

I returned home much easier in my mind. I locked the door behind me as I went in.

I took my cases up to the bedroom and found that the contents of the drawers in the bedroom and the wardrobe were the things Jed moved, obviously throwing the contents into my suitcases, but touching nothing else. However, the thought of his coarse hands touching my underclothes made me turn them all out. I found some hand wash and washed them in the bathroom. I rigged up a clothesline from a ball of string I found and hung them out to dry. It took quite a while to sort things out, but eventually it was done.

Later when they were dry, I ironed them and began to put things back in the drawers. One of the drawers still stuck, as though something was jamming it, so this time I pulled it out and felt behind it. To my surprise I found a pack of letters tied up in a pink ribbon. When I opened them I saw that they were letters addressed to Aunt Em interleaved with copies of her replies.

What should I do? Read them or just throw them away?

I stopped what I was doing and read them. They were love letters, tender and passionate, from Roger Flatley, obviously a soldier. Aunt Em's secret lover? They read like a love story but as I got to the end of them and read the copies of Aunt Em's letters to him, I realised that Aunt Em was writing but there were no replies. The last thing in the pile was an official document *missing in action*. The tears streamed down my face as I read it. No wonder Aunt Em never married.

I put the letters back in a neat pile, tied them again with the ribbon, putting them this time not at the back of the drawer but in one of the bottom drawers amongst my scarves and gloves.

To take my mind off the encounter with Jed Thompson, I brought my sketchpad in from the car and set about painting the waterfall in oils. I got so engrossed in the picture that I painted on into the night, only stopping to grab something to eat.

Next day Nancy arrived to clean. I gave her the spare key.

"Lock up when you're finished." I was about to tell her about my encounter with Jed when she interrupted me.

"I know about it, Mum told me. It must have been really scary. I'm going to lock the door inside while I'm working and I'll certainly lock up when I leave. Where do you want me to put the key?"

"Keep it for now. I've got a spare one. I'm going into Ambleside to find a locksmith and get the locks changed."

Nancy waved me off and then went quickly into the house.

I drove to Ambleside stopping at Stod's Garage. Bert was there. As I drove up I could see he looked worried. I wondered what was the matter.

"Is something wrong with the car?" he asked, as I got out.

"No, there was a problem with someone called Jed Thompson breaking into my house. I wanted to ask you where I could find a locksmith."

Bert wiped his hands on his overall. He looked relieved. "That Jed's a bad lot. You stay away from him. I see now why you want a locksmith. We don't often lock our doors in these parts, but if it's Jed you are worried about, then you go and see Alan Barder. Leave your car here and have a word with him. His shop is just down the road. He will do a good job for you at a reasonable price."

I walked down the road. The shop front was easy to spot, as it boasted that it could tackle any sort of lock problem. It could cut keys, replace watch batteries, and unlock mobile phones.

The shop bell tinkled as I entered. The shop gave the impression of being hit by a hurricane. Locks of all kinds were lying about. A key cutting machine stood in the corner, and there were safes of all kinds standing against the walls. As I came in, a small stocky man, quite old, entered from the back through a bead curtain and stood at the work bench looking at me through pebble glasses on the end of his nose.

"Are you Mr Barder?" I asked.

"Yes, how can I help?" He had a quiet voice.

"Mr Stod said I should come to you. I live in Little Tenderden and need my locks changing." I explained about Jed Thompson.

"I can see you need help quickly." He stroked his moustache thoughtfully. "I'll tell you what, I shall be shutting the shop shortly and will come straight away after that."

"That's very good of you. Here's the key to the door. Does that help?"

He examined the key carefully. "I've got a better lock than this in stock, so it should be easy to change." He gave the key back to me. "Let me have your address."

I took the key and wrote my address down for him.

I went back to the garage, thanked Bert, and as I knew Isobel Santir's address, I drove past it on my way home so that I would know where it was for the soiree the next evening.

True to his word, Alan Bader turned up at about six o'clock that evening, took one look at the lock and said, "That's no problem." He went to his van and brought out a new lock with two keys, fitting in no time at all.

"Do you want the back door done as well?" he asked.

"I hadn't thought of that, but yes please."

When he looked at it, he said, "This is quite a simple lock, let me fit you a better one."

I agreed, and when he finished I paid him and he went off assuring me that if there was any problem he was always willing to help.

I confess I felt much more secure after he left and the doors were safely locked.

Chapter Six

It was Thursday evening. Isobel's house was a grand mansion on the outskirts of Ambleside set in its own grounds. Feeling rather nervous, I drove up the short, gravelled drive and parked my car with a number of others in front of the house. Entrance was through a massive two pillared porch. I was half an hour late but judged that this would be about right to arrive. I debated whether to take a bottle of wine as a gift, but as this was my first visit and I didn't know the rules, I decided against it. Lights shone out from the downstairs windows and as I approached the front door I could hear sounds of merriment. I rang the bell and almost immediately the door was flung open and Isobel ushered me in.

"Come on in. Meet the gang. We have been working hard all day dealing with the visitors and now everyone is relaxing." She thrust a glass of champagne into my hand.

"Nibbles over there, but let me introduce you to one or two people." She guided me gently in the direction of a group of three men and a woman.

"Let me introduce Serina Spelton, an aspiring painter," she said.

I was surprised that she remembered my name, but there was no time to reflect on that as the group immediately surrounded me and began asking the usual questions.

After a while Isobel came back and led me into a corner alcove.

"I thought you needed rescuing. Talk to me for a bit and then we can turn you loose on some other people."

Isobel was the sort of person that you could confide in and before long I found myself telling the story of my life.

Then hesitating, I said, "I want to stay in the Lake District but I only have a limited amount of money and that's going to run out soon. I have to find a job, as painting isn't going to keep me."

In embarrassment, I looked around the high ceilinged room. The wall paper swirled with spread tailed peacocks, elaborate ferns and winged insects of many kinds. Around the walls statues stood in discreet alcoves where people were sitting talking. The one in which we sat was overlooked by a statue of a dancer.

Isobel saw me looking at it. "That was me in my youth. Sculpted by Enrico Gaselli. He was in love with me at the time. A nice boy." She sighed. "Ah, the moments of forgotten youth. But we must get back to your problem. You need a job, and I think I know just the person for you to talk to."

I was swept over to the small bar on the other side of the room where a tall, grey-haired man with piercing eyes stood surveying the assembled company with a look of amusement on his face.

"Charles, I want you to meet Serina Spelton. She's an artist and is looking for a job."

Taken aback by this direct approach I looked shyly at the man.

"Serina, let me introduce Charles Aventine. Charles, what do you think?"

Charles looked me up and down. "I like what I see. I think you will do, subject of course to qualifications."

Isobel turned to me. "Charles runs the major art gallery in the town and is looking for an assistant."

With no experience of getting a job, having gone to look after my father straight out of Art College, I was taken unawares. Was this the way it happened? I didn't think so, but this was exactly the sort of job I would want to take.

"I have no experience of working in an Art Gallery, but I have been to Art College and I would welcome the chance to try."

"There we are then. Now, no more business talk." Isobel turned and walked away to talk to a portly gentleman.

"Come to my gallery at nine o'clock in the morning and bring your certificates. Do you have a portfolio of paintings?" Charles Aventine asked.

"Only one painting I've done recently. It's of the local waterfall, but I have my work from Art College."

"Bring it all. Here's my card, I shall look forward to seeing you in the morning." With that he walked away and began to talk to Isobel and the portly gentleman.

Left alone I wandered about the room looking at the magnificent drapes covering the full length windows and admiring what looked like an Adam fireplace.

"Yes," said a voice. "It is an Adam fireplace. Nothing but the best for Isobel."

I turned, and there behind me was a slim well-dressed man with blue eyes similar to my own and a rather nice smile. He was holding what looked like a glass of whisky.

"I'm Paul Benson." He held out his hand.

As I shook it, a tingle ran up my arm and through my body. I staggered slightly.

"Are you all right?" he asked anxiously.

"I'm fine." I felt slightly faint. "I think I need to sit down for a minute."

We moved away from the fireplace and sat down in one of the alcoves.

"So what sort of painter are you?" he asked.

"I've only just started painting again after looking after an invalid father. How about you?"

"I'm a naturalistic painter, and you are going to ask me

what that is."

"Well, yes, does it mean that you paint natural things?"

"Not exactly, I paint using pigments from local rocks in my paintings."

"Such as?"

"Well, obviously charcoal for black, then I use pigments made from the large variety of coloured stones that can be found in this area."

"I buy my paints from Humbles. How can you make paints from stones?"

"If you are interested, I can show you. Why don't you come over to my workshop sometime?"

"I would love to, but I can't at the moment," I said regretfully. "I've an offer of a job and I have to report first thing in the morning."

We would have gone on talking but were interrupted by two lively girls, obviously twins as they not only looked alike but were dressed alike in crisp cotton dresses, their hair tied up with ribbons, one blue and one pink.

"Come on, Paul, you can't sit there all evening. It's time you played us a tune."

"I didn't know you were a musician as well as a painter," I said as they dragged him away.

"He's a man of many talents," one of them called over her shoulder.

They led him over to a rather *grand* grand piano.

He sat down and began to play a selection of Viennese waltzes. Men and women formed a crowd around him. Cut off in the middle of talking to him I felt bereft but couldn't really say why. The magic was gone out of the evening, so although I talked to one or two people after that, I soon gave my excuses to Isobel and made my way home.

Chapter Seven

Nine o'clock next morning, I presented myself at the Art Gallery, a large two fronted bow windowed showroom situated in a prominent position at the edge of the town.

A bell clanged as I went through the front door. A smell like turpentine mixed with another sweetish smell wafted over me. The pleasant room was filled with paintings, most of which looked like local scenes.

Charles Aventine came forward to greet me.

"I saw you looking at the paintings." He waved his hand. "Most of them are by local painters, but we keep a few specials for regular customers in the back room. They are never to be touched."

I thought it a bit strange that he should say that, as he hadn't even officially employed me yet, but it was obviously something in the forefront of his mind.

"Early morning is always a slack time," he said. "I usually use it to do some stocktaking but let me see what you have brought."

I was clutching my not yet framed painting of the falls. He took it and held it to the light.

"You have real talent. I would like to display this in the gallery, but first you must get it framed. Now what about your qualifications?"

I showed him my other work and certificates, and he seemed satisfied.

"What I need is someone to be here five days a week, you

can have Sunday and Monday off. I need you to receive paintings, show them to me for my decision, and then if we accept them you will catalogue them and display them for sale. We make a small percentage on every painting sold."

"Does that mean I have to actually sell things?" I began to feel anxious.

He smiled. "Don't worry, you will soon get used to it. I will train you in all the details."

After that we got on well, and I was soon drinking a cup of coffee with him in the back room, which was stacked with all manner of canvases, some covered carefully in brown paper.

"My previous assistant left to get married to the local doctor," he explained. "So you coming along at that particular moment was like manna from heaven."

After coffee we were in the middle of a training session on how to greet and be pleasant to a potential customer when the doorbell clanged and Paul Benson stood on the mat.

Advancing towards us holding a package, he stopped in his tracks as he saw me standing at the desk.

Charles stepped towards him.

"Hello, Charles." Paul looked at me. "I've just come to deliver another painting if you can handle it for me."

"Of course. But first let me introduce my new assistant. Serina, this is Paul Benson, a local artist."

For the second time we shook hands, with the same reaction.

"We met at Isobel Santir's soiree." I desperately tried to hold my voice steady. "I'm Serina Spelton, and I was hoping we would meet again."

Charles looked as though he could sense something between us. "Isobel's gatherings are always great fun. Let's see your picture."

Paul unwrapped the package, revealing a hillside scene.

"This is the view above Windemere isn't it?" Charles asked. "Has it got your usual piece of the Lake District in it?"

"Of course," Paul seemed not to be able to take his gaze off me. "We were talking last night about my work, and I invited Serina to see how I use the local stones. When would you be free?" he asked me.

I looked at Charles. " I start tomorrow, Saturday, right?"

He looked at me with a smile. "Yes, off you go, we've done enough for one day. I'll see you tomorrow at nine sharp."

"Thanks Charles, I'll be there." I knew then that I was going to enjoy the job and that I liked Charles Aventine very much.

Paul's car was a blue open two seater and he ushered me into it like royalty.

We drove a short distance and were soon at a rather dilapidated shed that stood in a farmyard surrounded by a number of other buildings in various states of repair.

"John Turner manages the farm." He handed me in through the door. "He lets me have a small cottage round the corner and the use of this barn for a very small rent."

I looked around. The barn was obviously used to store farm machinery. An old tractor stood in the far corner, there were bales of hay, and on the wall over a bench, a variety of tools, most of which I couldn't recognise.

"Over here." He led me to a larger bench on which I could see jars of coloured liquid and a jar with brushes stuck in it haphazardly. There were some large chunks of rock and a number of smaller pots containing a variety of pebbles.

"You don't see the colours properly until you wet them. Look, I'll show you."

He took what I thought was a particularly unattractive piece of light blue stone, poured water over it from a jug, and all at once it turned a magnificent deep blue colour.

"Incredible." I almost couldn't believe my eyes.

"This is quite a rare stone. The others are easy to get hold of, but I've only found this in one place, I'll show you sometime if you like."

"Do you dig them out of the ground?"

"Sometimes, but mostly I knock bits of the rocks with my Swiss Army Knife. It's got all sorts of gadgets on it."

He showed me other stones, and I was amazed at the range of colours, yellows, browns, red and purple, stones of all shapes and sizes.

I looked at him in wonder. "How do you make them into paints?"

"Secret formula." He laughed. "No, not really, just a lot of hard work. You have to grind bits off and then mix the bits with turpentine to make a paste. I paint landscapes in oils, so anyone who buys a local scene is actually getting a real piece of the Lake District built into the picture."

He showed me some of the canvases standing against the wall.

"That's amazing. What made you think of doing this?"

He leant back against the table. "I saw a film of John Glenn where he told how he incorporated moon dust in his paintings. It set me thinking, and I realised I could do it with rocks from this planet. Would you like me to show you where I get the blue stone from? It comes from the top of a waterfall. It's not exactly a secret place. I think it is the only source of it, but I can show you."

"I look forward to it, but it will have to wait awhile as I have to settle into my new job."

"Can we share phone numbers? I would like to keep in touch. Here's my number."

I thought for a minute then decided that I wanted to see more of him, so there was no harm in it. "Best if I give you my mobile number."

We exchanged numbers, and as I turned, he put his hand on my shoulder. I suddenly felt a longing that I hadn't felt for a long time. He put his arms round me and our lips met, rousing a passion in me that I thought was dead.

We both looked at each other in astonishment. I pulled away and ran to the door.

"Wait, wait," he called. "I must drive you home."

In his car we sat in silence as though conscious that something momentous had happened between us.

When we got to the house and before I got out of the car, I said in a choked up voice, "Do you want to come in?"

He shook his head. "I'd better not but I must see you again soon." He rested his hand lightly on my thigh. I knew then that I wanted this man.

Chapter Eight

As I got out of the car and waved him off, my mind was full of conflicting thoughts. My body suddenly came alive—something not felt since sex with Terry.

"Oh, bother," I said aloud as I walked into the house. "This isn't one of your romantic novels, just take it as it comes." But then I thought, when would I see him again, and next time what would happen?

I went to bed and fell asleep with all sorts of erotic images in my mind.

Next day at the gallery I hoped Paul would come in or at least would phone me, but he didn't. I could feel the tension in my body, but I had to concentrate on my work.

There were a number of visitors during the day. Most wanted to browse the pictures and not buy anything, but there were also some genuine buyers. I was delighted to sell one of Paul's paintings, which came with a certificate from him certifying that it contained genuine parts of rocks from the area.

"Paul is a clever young man," Charles said when I told him of the sale. "Keep up the good work."

And I did. In the next few days I developed a technique with the visitors where I would greet them and try to calm their fears at walking into a strange environment and not wanting to buy anything. I then pointed out some of the pictures to them and made sales often enough to delight Charles.

"I wish you had been with me earlier," he said.

I soon felt completely settled in, but for some reason there was no phone call from Paul. Why was he keeping away from me?

On Thursday as I was packing up after work, I determined to phone Paul when I got home to find out why he was avoiding me.

When I turned into my drive and got out of the car, Jed Thompson was standing near the house. When he saw me, he advanced and grabbed my arm. I dropped my handbag.

"Thought you were going to get away with it?" he said.

"Stop it, Jed, you're hurting my arm,"

He began dragging me towards the house.

"I'll teach you to take my house away from me." I remembered lessons in Jujitsu learnt at College. I twisted round, getting his arm behind him. I kicked his feet from under him so that he fell to his knees, but he was so powerful that he was soon up and grabbing me again.

I wasn't sure what happened next. It seemed as though a whirlwind struck.

Jed was thrown to the ground and a figure dressed in khaki battledress stood over him. With a snarl Jed got to his feet and threw himself at the newcomer, who sidestepped and Jed went flying.

"Get out and stay out." The figure planted a hefty kick and Jed again sprawled in the mud. "Get going before I change my mind and give you a thrashing."

Jed rose slowly onto one knee. He gave us a look of sheer malevolence, got to his feet, and made off shaking his fist.

The figure turned itself into Roy Blinks.

"We met the other day at the shop. I was just coming up to ask if you wanted another walk when I saw you were having more trouble with Jed Thompson."

I brushed myself down. "Thank you, Roy. I am grateful for

the rescue. Rather than a walk, would you care to come in for a cup of tea?"

"Love one," he said.

Picking up my bag I noticed a tattoo on his left arm that looked somehow familiar.

"I'm going to have to clean my bag after this." I brushed off the dirt, taking the keys and opening the door. "Come on in."

I was still a bit shaken but led the way inside and settled Roy down in one of the armchairs while I went into the kitchen to make the tea.

"I'm sorry Jed Thompson is bothering you like this," he said. "He's a right bad lot. Into all sorts of crooked games. I'll give you my phone number. Let me know if he bothers you again."

Roy Blinks was an oldish man, but he held himself well and from that and his dress I assumed that he had been in the army.

Later over tea he confirmed this.

"After the war I was invalided out of the army."

"You're not old enough to have been in the war."

He laughed. "Not World War Two. This was the Falklands war. I was hit on the head by a piece of shrapnel and lost my memory, but after I got out of hospital there was a strange compulsion to come back to this part of the world. I don't know why I'm telling you this, but we are near neighbours."

"What about your neighbours apart from Jed Thompson?" I asked.

"Well, there's only old Ted Barnes and Rosy Profit. They keep to themselves mostly."

"I've met Ted. He's offered to keep the garden tidy."

"I believe he used to do that for Miss Renault. He's a nice enough chap, likes his pint, but I'm sure he's a good worker. Rosy Profit, now there's a one. Used to be a well- known painter, so I'm told, never married, and came out here to hide herself. I see her occasionally down at the village shop, but that's about all." He finished his tea and put the cup down. "Well, after all that excitement I won't press you to go for a walk. Let me know if you ever need any help." He swung his walking stick in the air as if hitting an imaginary opponent.

I saw him to the door and waved goodbye.

It was now too late to phone Paul, and I felt totally drained after my encounter with Jed Thompson so I made myself a hasty meal and sat reading until it was time for bed.

Chapter Nine

Next day after breakfast I phoned Paul's number, but there was no reply. I mentally kicked myself. I mustn't chase this man—let things take their course.

To take my mind off it, I went out into the garden where Ted Barnes was working. As he saw me he straightened up and leant on his spade.

"Morning, Mam. Lovely day." Then fumbling in his pocket, he held something out. "I've just found this. It was in the vegetable patch where I was doing some deep digging."

He handed me what looked like a lump of metal encrusted in dirt.

"What is it?" I asked.

"I think it's something from the war. A badge of some kind."

"Come on in the house, we can wash the dirt off."

"Thank you kindly, Mam, but I wouldn't like to dirty your floor with my boots." He shuffled uncomfortably. "You take it and give it a wash." He touched his cap and made off down the garden.

"The garden is looking good," I called after him.

I took the object and washed it under the tap. It was a badge of some kind. The design on it looked familiar.

Where have I seen this before?

I dried it with a piece of kitchen paper, washed my hands. I wrapped the badge in paper and slipped it in my handbag.

Perhaps Paul would know what it is. This gives me an excuse to phone him.

Before I left for work, I phoned. This time he answered his

phone.

"Paul, if you're free, can you come over to the gallery sometime today? There's something I need your opinion on."

I thought he sounded a bit strained, but he said, "Yes, of course. How about if I come over at lunchtime? We could have a snack at the teashop just down the road."

"That sounds fine. My break is from one till two."

I could hear warmth coming back into his voice. "I'll be there."

The teashop was the old-fashioned kind with tablecloths and waitresses in frilly aprons. We sat at a corner table. I ordered a ham sandwich and Earl Grey tea with lemon. Paul ordered a cheese and pickle sandwich and a coffee.

As we waited for our food, I was about to ask him why he hadn't been in touch when he brought the subject up himself.

Looking guilty he said, "I expect you wondered why I haven't phoned you?"

"Well, yes. Especially after that moment in your workshop."

"I wanted to." He reached across the table and held my hand. "But I wasn't sure if you felt the same way I did, and I didn't want to make the same mistake twice."

"What do you mean?"

The sandwiches and drinks arrived, and he went quiet for a moment.

Then he said, "It's a long story. I made a disastrous marriage a long time ago. I won't go into it now, but after my divorce I vowed not to make the same mistake again. Then you came along."

We ate our sandwiches in companionable silence.

Then I said, "I almost forgot the reason for phoning you." I took the badge out of my handbag and handed it to him. "My gardener found this when he was digging. I wondered if you knew what it was?"

He put his cup down and turned the badge over carefully in his hand. "It's an Army Cap Badge. I'm not sure which regiment, but you can easily find out. I'm sure there is a book in the library that will tell you. Have you met our librarian, Enid Minton? She helped me find a book on local minerals. Go and see her after work. The library stays open quite late. I could meet you there if you like."

"Thanks, Paul. I would like that. See you there at about six." I put the badge back in my handbag.

After work that evening I went to the library. It was an impressive building quite near to the gallery. I went in and looked around for Paul, but there was no sign of him.

A small grey-haired old lady in a green apron clutching a pile of books came up to me. "Can I help you? You look lost."

"I was supposed to meet a friend here, but he must have been delayed."

"I'm sure he will turn up. Did you want to look for something in particular?" she asked.

"Yes, I've come to ask if you have any reference books on Army badges."

"We should have, I'm Enid Minton, the librarian here. Excuse the books, so many people return their books on a Friday, and we have to put them back on the shelves for the weekend." She put the books down on a desk and signalled one of her assistants to take over while she led me to the reference section.

I looked around at the array of shelves packed with books. "You have a fantastic collection of books."

Enid smiled. "Yes, we are lucky to be one of the main libraries in the area. Of course we have a mobile library that goes to the outlying districts, but it doesn't have as comprehensive a selection as we have here. Let's have a look to see what we can find."

"It's very kind of you to help me, especially as you must be busy preparing for the weekend."

"Don't mention it. It's a pleasure to welcome a new face. Now what about this badge?"

I felt in my handbag and brought out the badge.

"It looks like a cap badge." She pulled out a volume. "Badges of the British Army, that should do it." She turned over the pages. "Here we are. Look, it's the badge of a special parachute regiment. What's the story behind it?"

"My gardener found it when he was digging in the garden. I don't know how it got there."

"Troops were billeted all around here in the war. It probably got dropped and buried in the soil."

A sudden memory flashed across my mind. "I'm sure I have seen this design before, but I can't think where."

As I thanked her for her help and turned to go, Paul dashed in.

"Sorry I'm late. The car got a puncture, so I walked."

"All that distance."

"It's not far. Did you find what you were looking for?"

"Yes, Enid was very helpful. Come on, I'll give you a lift back to your place. The car is outside."

"What about your puncture?" I asked as we reached the farm.

"I'll get it fixed, no problem. More importantly, when can I see you again?"

I felt the tension in my body. "How about tomorrow night as it's Saturday? Come to dinner."

He bent over and gave me a quick kiss on the cheek. "I'll be there. What time?"

"About seven thirty." I waved as he drove off.

Chapter Ten

When I got back home, the memory of the badge still bothered me and then I remembered there was a drawing of a badge in one of Aunt Em's love letters. I took the bundle of letters out of the drawer and went through them looking for the drawing. There it was, near the beginning of the bundle. I compared it with the badge. It was identical.

I replaced the letter in the bundle and sat down to think. The drawing was also identical to the tattoo on Roy Blinks' arm. If he served in the same regiment as Aunt Em's sweetheart then he should know him. I decided to call on Roy and ask him.

Taking the badge and Aunt Em's letters I went down to Roy Blink's cottage.

Roy greeted me.

"I know it's late, but could I talk to you for a bit?" I asked.

"Of course, make yourself at home."

I looked around the room. It was a man's room. Everything was squared away and tidy, but it lacked a woman's touch and was severely masculine.

"What can I do for you?" he asked as we sat down on opposite sides of his well-scrubbed kitchen table.

"I wanted to show you this." I put the cap badge and the letters on the table, and pushed the badge across to him.

He picked it up, turning it over in his hand. "That's odd." He looked down at the tattoo on his arm. "Where did you get this?"

"Ted Barnes found it in my garden, and even odder. Look

at this." I opened the bundle of letters, selected one and opened it at the drawing. "I shouldn't really show you these letters as they were between my Aunty Em and her sweetheart during the war. His name was Roger Flatley and he was reported missing, but it's such a coincidence. You must have been in the same regiment. Do you remember Roger Flatley?"

Roy looked puzzled. "I don't remember anything before I was in hospital, but" – he paused – "the name does sound familiar." He looked again at the badge and the letter then, to my surprise, he put his head in his hands, while leaning forwards over the table.

I was alarmed. "Are you all right?" I asked, coming round the table.

Roy raised his head and looked at me. "It's all coming back," he said. "Just flashes. Was your Aunt called Emily Renault?"

"Yes she was," I sat down abruptly on a chair. "How did you know that?"

"Because, I think I'm Roger. We were very much in love and were going to get married after the war but I was injured, lost my memory and never came back here until now." Tears came to his eyes. "Seeing my handwriting brought it all back to me." His head dipped into his arms again.

I put my arm round his shoulders. I was surprised at this sudden change in him, he seemed a different person.

"It's all coming back. I was a bank manager before the war and I collected paintings. Emily promised to look after them for me when I was called up."

I felt a surge of emotion. So this was my aunt's sweetheart. Aunt Em hadn't known he was alive, and now she was gone.

Roy or Roger looked up. "I need to think this through. Do you mind if I spend a bit of time on my own?"

"Of course. Would you like me to leave the letters with you?"

"Yes please," he said, clutching them. "Can I contact you tomorrow?"

"Make it Sunday, as I will be here all day. Come up to the house when you're ready."

He looked up, holding the bundle of letters. "Thank you," he said.

Paul arrived at exactly seven thirty that evening. I heard the sound of tires on gravel as he drew up outside the front door.

I was in the kitchen finishing preparations for the meal. When I heard the bell, I quickly took off my apron to reveal my open neck blouse and short skirt. I raced to the front door.

Paul thrust a bunch of roses into my hands as I opened the door. "You look gorgeous." He bent forwards and kissed me lightly on the cheek. It would have been nice to have a proper kiss, but perhaps that would come later.

"Come in." I held the roses up and smelt the wafting scent. "Hmm, my favourite flower."

I led him into the sitting room and took his coat. He was dressed in an open necked shirt and slacks. "A drink before dinner?" I asked, putting the roses down on a side table.

I could see that Paul wasn't sure how to answer. I felt like a teenager on my first date and I'm sure he felt the same.

"What are you having?" he asked tentatively.

"I'll just have a glass of wine. I don't drink spirits, but I know you do. I saw you drinking whisky at Isobel's soiree."

Paul went red in the face with embarrassment. "I'm afraid Isobel spoiled me. I told her I didn't like punch, so she brought me something stronger. Could I have some whisky? But I like to take it with water."

I went out and came back with a tumbler of whisky and a jug of water. "Take this while I go and put these lovely roses in water."

When I returned holding a glass of wine, he said, "I like the paintings. Are they yours?"

I looked down shyly. "I did them mostly at college. I thought they would brighten the place up a bit." I could feel the tension between us.

We talked about things generally to cover the awkward silence. How was my car? Was I settled in? I hastened to find something else that might intrigue him. I remembered the locked door in the second bedroom. I was about to tell him about it when the rich aroma of cooking wafted in from the kitchen.

I gasped. "I must go to the kitchen, or our meal will be ruined."

Paul followed me and I was just in time to rescue the leg of lamb before it burnt. I placed it on a carving dish.

"Are you any good at carving? Because I'm not. My father once told me when I was trying to carve a chicken that I might as well take it out into the road and let a steamroller run over it."

Paul laughed and took the proffered carving knife. "I'm better at wielding a brush, but I'll have a go."

I admired the way he took the knife and firmly cut thin slices instead of the chunks that I would have hacked off.

"There. Now it's your turn to turn the rest of the meal into a work of art."

The awkwardness between us seemed to have passed.

We sat for a long time over the meal. The wine was a Rioja.

"This is very smooth." He raised his glass. "It tastes of vibrant summer fruits and spicy vanilla flavours."

"How did you know that?" I asked.

"I read it on the bottle." He laughed.

I gave him a sharp tap on the shoulder. "That's for faking it."

"I will never fake it with you," he said, looking into my eyes.

I felt myself colouring up. I turned away. "I must get the dessert."

Paul rose to help me.

I motioned him to sit down. "I'll do it. Won't be a minute."

The sweet was Eve's pudding, tempting apples hidden under a sponge topping with a little vanilla ice-cream.

After the meal, we relaxed in the sitting room in front of a blazing log fire. I brought in coffee and chocolates.

"A perfect meal," Paul said, stretching out his legs to the warmth. "And a perfect hostess."

I looked across at him and thought how handsome he looked and wondered what it would be like to live with a man like this.

Neither of us spoke for a while, just glorying in each other's company until I remembered I was going to tell him about the locked door. "There's a mystery about this house."

"Not a ghost story," he said. "I know all good evenings should end with a ghost story but if you have a ghost, I don't want to hear about it."

I laughed. "No, nothing to worry about, it's just a bit strange. It's just a locked door in the spare bedroom."

Paul was now all attention. "You can't open it and you think there may be something nasty behind it?"

"I wish you hadn't put thought into my head, but it is a door I can't open. There's a keyhole, but I can't find the key anywhere."

"Do you want me to take a look? I might be able to open it."

I felt a bit diffident about letting Paul go upstairs but quickly reasoned that it was only the spare room so it didn't matter. We climbed the steep cottage stairs.

"It's the room on the right-hand side."

I realised as we went up that the door of my own bedroom was open and my nightdress was spread invitingly out on the bed. Would he take that as an invitation? Something wild possessed me and I thought, I don't care if he does. I trembled with excitement as I opened the spare room door and switched on the light. The room still possessed its original wallpaper, a muddy brown scattered with futuristic looking flowers.

"Very tasteful!" Paul said mockingly.

I looked steadily at him. "I haven't got around to redecorating it yet."

"Sorry, I was just being facetious."

"The door is over there." I pointed to the corner.

Paul took out his Swiss army knife and opened one of the gadgets on it. "This might do the trick. I mustn't force it. Ah, that's it."

I don't know how he did it, but the lock yielded.

He gave a firm push, and the door was open. More stairs. Paul brushed away the cobwebs. A dim light filtered into the dusty attic room that was revealed.

"Wait, I've got a torch." I went to my bedroom to fetch it.

"Come on up," he said as he stooped under the roof space.

I went up and we both stood for a moment surveying the room. Over in one corner there were a number of large, thin, dusty packages. I shone my torch around the room.

"No-one has been up here for years," he said.

I looked around. The moonlight filtered in through a cobwebby skylight.

"There's almost room for another bedroom up here, but it's a bit gloomy."

"Hold still." He gripped me round the waist, brushing away a large spider that had landed on my shoulder. He swung me towards him. His grip tightened. Our lips met.

Then he backed away rapidly. "Sorry, I don't know what came over me." He pointed to the skylight. "It must have been the moon."

"No need to be sorry, I rather enjoyed it."

"In that case." This time there was no doubt. We both surrendered to our feelings.

"Let's go downstairs," I said breathlessly.

I climbed back down into the bedroom, his hands still gripping my waist.

As he came down he lifted me onto the single bed that the room contained.

I raised my hands, thrusting him away, "No, not here. Come into my room."

CHAPTER ELEVEN

I led the way across, rapidly throwing my nightdress off the bed and onto a chair.

I lay back on the bed as he lay beside me. His hand fumbled with the top button of my blouse.

"Here, let me do it," I laughed, rapidly undoing the blouse and shrugging it off.

He gripped my shoulders and gently pushed me back on the bed. His lips met mine in a passionate kiss as he slid the straps of my brassiere down. He pulled back for a moment, ripping his shirt off as I unfastened my bra and tossed it on the chair.

In a moment his lips caressed my breasts. A thrill of anticipation ran through me like a lightning bolt.

His kisses edged lower on my body as I wriggled out of my skirt.

I tugged at his slacks, pulling the zip down. In seconds he was as naked as I was, apart from my pink knickers, which he eased away from my skin.

"Take them off," I breathed as he pulled them down stroking my legs as he did so.

His mouth was on mine but his hands were elsewhere. I heard the rustle of a condom, then he thrust into me slowly and rhythmically. In a moment of sheer delight we came together and lay exhausted on the bed.

I don't know how much time passed, as I must have fallen asleep. When I woke Paul was just coming back from the bathroom. His powerful body rippled in the light as he slipped on his briefs, his slacks and shirt.

I lay stretched out naked on the bed. He leant over and kissed me gently as I held out my hands to him.

Some time later I washed and dressed. Paul emerged from the spare bedroom carrying one of the packages from the attic room.

"I thought I would take another look at those packages while I waited for you. I've left the others but brought this one down as it has a letter attached to it."

"Let's close up the attic door and go downstairs, it will be warmer there." I was feeling it difficult to switch back to reality.

Once in the kitchen I could see that the picture was carefully packed in brown paper and sealed with tape.

"Let me have a kitchen knife," he said. "No, wait. Have you got a duster? Let's do things properly."

After dusting the package down he carefully slit the securing tape and pulled the paper away. A riot of colour hit my eyes as the picture was revealed sparkled in the artificial light.

It was a rural scene with maidens sitting on a riverbank, some in the water bathing nude, and above them on a bridge, a figure on horseback looked down.

"I don't know the painting, but it looks valuable. I wonder what else we shall find up there. But, first, you should open the letter." The envelope was still attached to the brown paper.

"You open it, Paul. I'm a bit overwhelmed,"

"It's a letter from your aunt to you." He carefully unfolded the pages. "Here, you must read it."

"It is from Aunt Em." I was hardly able to take my gaze away from the magnificent picture.

"What does it say?" Paul asked eagerly.

"It's a letter about my aunt's wartime sweetheart. He was killed in the war, but apparently he loved paintings and although he didn't have a lot of money to spare, he bought paintings whenever he could. He left the paintings here with my Aunt to keep until they could get married and set up house together, but of course he never came back. But I know the sequel. Her sweetheart is alive and living just down the road. He lost his memory but came back to this area. I must tell him what we have found. Although Aunt Em says she was leaving everything to me, now we have found them, he must have them back."

"What a fantastic story. What do you want to do?"

"I truly don't know at the moment, I'm a bit overwhelmed."

We sat at the table, the painting gleaming at us.

"I suppose we ought to look at the other pictures," I said.

"Let me take a duster up, clean them off and bring them down and you can have a proper look at them."

I made to get up, but Paul said, "No, you stay here, I'll do it."

There were six paintings in all including the first one. I peeled the coverings off as Paul brought them down one by one. A treasure house was revealed. There were paintings of noblemen, society beauties, religious scenes and one obviously Dutch showing a couple standing by a door looking out.

"They must be worth a considerable amount of money. Your Aunt's sweetheart is going to be very pleased."

"Let's wrap them up in something. We could put them back in the spare bedroom until I can contact him. I've got a couple of old sheets we could use."

We wrapped them up and put them in the spare bedroom. The intensity of our lovemaking had been such that I suddenly felt drained of energy and when I looked at Paul I could see he felt the same.

He gave me a hug. "I think I ought to go, otherwise who knows what might happen."

I caressed his cheek. "I agree, all I want to do now is fall into bed and sleep. Can we meet again soon? I get Sundays and Mondays off from the gallery."

CHAPTER TWELVE

On Sunday morning I was washing up the breakfast things when there was a knock on the door. My first thought was it was Paul. I opened the door, and it was Roy Blinks.

He came clutching the letters.

"Can I keep these?" he asked. "I am Roger. I know that now I've read the letters, but I was very upset by her later letters when I saw that she got no reply. Thank you for helping me to bring my memory back, but it's all too late isn't it?"

"Come and sit down. It must have been a considerable shock." I made him a cup of tea and offered him a chocolate biscuit which he took gratefully.

"Did you find any of my paintings in the house?" he asked.

"Yes, we did. A friend was with me last night and we discovered six of them in the attic, along with a letter from Aunt Em to me telling your story."

"That's marvellous," he said.

"Do you want to see them?"

He thought for a moment. "I'm a bit overwhelmed at present. As long as I know they are safe. Perhaps I can come and collect them in a day or so?"

"Of course, any time. I've put them in my spare bedroom. They will be safe there until you want them."

He went off looking happy.

Paul rang me soon after. "I've been thinking. You told me you want to paint waterfalls, so I thought you ought to have a guided tour of some of them. How about coming out with me today, you said you get today off, so I could show you the sights."

"I'd love that. It's a good idea as I have only explored one or two."

"You can also be as touristy as you like."

I could tell from his tone of voice that he was pleased.

"Is there any particular place you would like to visit?"

"Dove cottage for Wordsworth, but that's Ambleside, so I could go there at any time. The other house I would really like to visit is Beatrix Potter's house at Near Sawry. I used to devour her stories when I was young."

"Right. I'll plan an itinerary starting with Far Sawry and then on the waterfall trail. When can I pick you up?"

"I'm tidying up. Just come when you are ready."

"That's fine, I'll be there."

"Shall I make a picnic?" I asked.

"No, we'll have lunch out on the way and then see how the day goes. See you soon."

True to his word he rolled up in his old blue coupe just as I finished washing the breakfast things and Roger's cup.

I invited him in. "Give me a minute to finish getting ready."

"Wear stout shoes if you have them. We shall be doing some walking up to the waterfalls."

I was already wearing jeans and a sweater so I slipped on a pair of stout shoes.

"Ready," I said, and we went out to the car. I locked the house door carefully, mindful of Jed Thompson.

"We'll go to Far Sawry first, then on to a waterfall in Satterthwaite forest. Here's a map so you can follow the route." He opened a map atlas, found the right page and handed it to me.

Before looking at the map I settled down in the seat beside him and stole a glance at his face, looking admiringly at his firm jaw and the laughter lines at the side of his blue eyes.

He sensed that I was looking at him and smiled.

I quickly put my head down and studied the map. "I see we go through Hawkshead on the way."

"Yes, it's full of things to see but also very full of tourists. Do you want to stop?"

"Not if it's teeming with tourists."

"Well, I can give you a brief tour guide. Wordsworth was educated at the Grammar School there and Beatrix Potter married the local solicitor."

"Enough. Let's get on to the house."

The road wound through glorious countryside. The sun shone down benevolently, and I felt at peace with the world. "The Lake District gives you a tremendous feeling of freedom. I love it here."

Paul nodded, not taking his gaze off the road. "I feel the same, but then I was born here."

"I didn't know that. Whereabouts?"

"Up near Rydal water. I plan to take you up there this afternoon if we have time."

We arrived at Hill Top, Beatrix Potter's house, and found it full of tourists. Paul paid the admission fee and we entered the typical stone-walled Lake District building, through the entrance hall straight into the parlour, where there was a grandfather clock.

"I recognise that clock," I said. "It's in one of the stories." Then a little later, "here's the coronation teapot."

We went up the stairs to the landing. The going was a bit difficult due to the press of people.

"She obviously put all the things in the house into her stories. I think I even recognise the carpets?"

We struggled down the stairs again, looked at each other and with a nod from me went back out to the car.

As we drove away, I said, "That was a thrill, thank you. I

used to read her books avidly, The Tale of Peter Rabbit, Jemima Puddle-Duck, oh, lots of them."

I settled contentedly in the passenger seat. The countryside began with rolling fields, distant hills and glimpses of sparkling water, and then began to turn into a birch tree forest.

Paul parked in a side lane off the main road. "This is our next stop. We have to walk up to the waterfall and it may be rough going, so take care."

He held my hand as I stumbled at first over exposed tree roots. Then the going got smoother as we forged on towards the waterfall.

When we reached it, hand in hand we stood looking up at the powerful water pouring down, splitting at the top round a huge chunk of rock and then cascading down in a series of steps until it reached the calmer waters of the river beneath.

"Spectacular." I freed my shoe from a bramble that threatened to trip me up.

"This is the farthest part of our trip. Do you want to stay awhile?" Paul took my hand again. "If not, I would suggest some refreshment. We go back through Hawkshead, so we could stop there if you like."

We walked back to the car and set off.

As we reached Hawkshead I took one look at the teeming mass of tourists and said, "I don't think we should stop here, it looks too busy."

"You're right," he said. " It's a pity, as there is a Beatrix Potter Gallery in the offices of the solicitor she married, William Heelis."

"Perhaps we can come back again?"

"Yes, let's do that. I know a good restaurant at Skelwich Bridge. How about going straight there, as it ties in nicely with the rest of our tour?"

"I agree, let's press on."

I settled back in my seat contentedly. *I feel comfortable with him in a way that I never have with a man before.*

Paul turned and smiled at me almost as though he could read my thoughts.

We arrived at Skelwich Bridge and entered the restaurant. We were lucky to get a table, as it was full of people dressed in walking gear.

"It is a popular place," Paul said. "I ought to have booked a table, but we were lucky."

Like two lovers, we sat facing each other and ate our meal in companionable silence. Paul paid the bill and we went to the car.

"I've been thinking. I was planning to show you Dungeon Ghyll Force at Great Langdale. That one is a really impressive waterfall and Wordsworth wrote about it in his poem *The Idle Shepherd Boys,* but I really want to show you Rydal Falls where I spent my childhood, and now that I think about it that will probably take us the rest of the day."

"You said that's where your parents live. Are we going to see them?"

Paul hesitated. "Well, not exactly."

"You mean you don't want your parents to see me." I tossed my head.

"Nothing like that. In fact I think they would approve of you. I suppose I shall have to tell you the whole sordid story."

We sat in the car park while Paul told me about Carlotta Boskoni, his disastrous marriage with her and how he came back to his roots after their divorce.

I put my hand over his in sympathy.

"My father disapproved of the marriage and warned me in no uncertain terms that it would be a disaster, but I ignored him. So you see, I can't go back to see them."

"Why not? After all, he might be delighted that you have broken away from her. People do like being right."

"But it's a loss of face for me." Paul's face twisted in misery.

I paused for a moment. "Come on, let's go to Rydal."

Paul looked relieved and thoughtful. "I'll show you our house anyway, it's near Rydal Water."

The road from Skelwich bridge led back to Ambleside, then on a byroad to Rydal Water. Paul stopped the car by the side of the lake.

"It's only a small lake. Probably one of the smallest in the Lake District, but over there"—he pointed—"are some steps leading to what they call *Wordsworth's Seat*. It was supposed to be where he sat overlooking the lake. He lived in the house Rydal Mount for a time. There's also Rydal Hall, which is the grand house in the area. I ought to take you there. We can get into the gardens and then up to the waterfalls. It's got a five-hundred-year-old sweet chestnut tree . . ."

I gave him a friendly push. "Stop acting like a tour guide and show me your house."

"It's a bit farther on." Then he pointed. "There it is, Campeston House. It has rolling lawns down to the lake. An ideal playground for my sister Susan and me when we were young."

"Let's go and surprise your parents."

"I've been thinking about that as we came along. Yes, all right, but I can't guarantee what sort of reception we shall get just barging in on them."

"The house looks like something straight out of a Jane Austen novel. Come on, let's go."

Chapter Thirteen

We drove through a grove of trees and up the gravel driveway to the house. Paul parked the car by the front door. As he got out, the oak studded front door opened and a white-haired woman dressed in a gardener's overall carefully descended the steps followed by a floppy-eared Labrador.

"Paul!" she said as he ran towards her. She held out her hands to him.

"Mother, it's lovely to see you."

"What are you doing here after all these years? We thought you were lost to us forever."

"No, you haven't, but it's a long story."

I was standing quietly behind Paul.

"Mother, meet Serina, a friend of mine." He bent down to fondle the ears of the Labrador. "Hello Tigger," he said.

I moved forwards and shook hands formally.

"Pleased to meet you, my dear. I'm Lucinda Benson. Come on in and meet Artero, my husband. I've been gardening, but we were just about to have some tea. Will you join us?"

I noticed Lucinda looking approvingly at me. *She thinks I'm an improvement on his ex-wife.*

We went into the house. I took in the wide entrance hall, its portraits, perhaps of ancestors? We turned into a comfortably furnished sitting room with leather armchairs and a settee in front of a cheerful blazing fire.

"Artero, darling look who's here," she said as we entered.

A thick-set man turned towards us. Grey hair, bushy eyebrows, a finely chiselled face and a commanding presence.

"Hello, son," he said as though Paul just walked in from the garden instead of being away for a number of years. "And who is this?" He looked critically at me. I could see that his eyes were taking in every detail.

"I'm Serina Spelton." I advanced towards him, and shook his hand.

"I'll get the tea." Lucinda made for the door.

"Let me come with you." I hurried to help.

"Good idea to leave these two together for a bit." Lucinda led the way to the kitchen.

Lucinda was obviously curious about me. She asked, "Have you known Paul long?"

"No, not long. Long enough to know that you have a caring son."

"Not caring enough," Lucinda said bitterly. "After his marriage to that woman . . . do you know about that?"

"Yes, Paul told me."

"After that he didn't come to see us. I know it was his father that sent him away, but before that we were so close." Lucinda looked at me in an embarrassed way. "I don't know why I'm telling you this, my dear. Let's go back to the men."

Over tea Paul talked about his decision to come back to the Lake District.

"Why has it taken all this time for you to come to see us?" Artero asked.

"It was Serina, really," Paul said, turning to me. "I did make a mistake marrying Carlotta but couldn't admit it to you. Today I was showing Serina around the area and she persuaded me to come to see you. I'm glad I did."

Lucinda squeezed his hand. "And so are we, aren't we Artero?"

"Hmm, young fool," Artero grunted. " Of course we are pleased to see you. Anyway, you're back now thanks to this young lady." He took a swift look in my direction.

"Now you're here, how about staying for dinner?" Lucinda asked.

Paul looked at me. "What do you think? I promised to show you the waterfall where I used to play. We go up past Rydal Hall which is just nearby. It won't take long."

"We would love to stay," I said. "You have a lovely house and I've been admiring your pictures." I pointed to what looked like a Constable over the fireplace and other equally notable paintings round the walls.

Lucinda smiled. "Artero is an art critic, my dear. Don't tell me you're a painter as well as Paul?"

"Yes, but just a beginning one."

"That's settled then. You two go and enjoy yourselves. Come back when you're ready."

We walked out onto the road and Paul indicated a narrow lane. "That's Rydal Hall over there." He pointed to the right. "We are now on the coffin road."

I shuddered. "Why is it called that?"

"They used to take the coffins up this way to the graveyard in Grasmere, but that was a long time ago."

We went through a kissing gate and into a wood. For a moment Paul looked as though he was going to lean over the gate and kiss me. I sensed this and held myself ready but at the last minute he turned away.

To hide my confusion I said, "I can hear the sound of the falls already."

"There are two of them. The best is at the top. We go over the river on this bridge. This is the first one. Then up the hill."

We reached the top. Water cascaded down in two magnificent falls.

I breathed in the spray. "Fantastic." I looked around—the setting was wonderful. I again felt a sense of freedom and looked across at Paul as though seeing him for the first time.

"I used to play here as a child. Susan, my sister, and I were allowed to go into Rydal Hall. You can make your way up to the falls through their gardens. It was a good place to grow up in."

We retraced our steps.

Paul reached out and held my hand. "So you don't slip on the muddy path."

It gave me a great feeling of togetherness. I felt we were one and I liked his parents.

We returned to Paul's parents' house.

"Just in time for drinks," Lucinda greeted us as we came in.

Artero beamed at us. "I hope you will visit more often." Then he said to me, " Now what will you have?"

"Gin and tonic please." I looked at Paul, wondering why his father hadn't asked him as well.

Artero caught my look. "Whisky as usual, Paul?"

"Thanks Dad, you remembered."

Artero handed me my gin and tonic.

"Where are you staying?" Lucinda asked Paul.

"I've got a cottage at John Turner's place."

"Is old John still going?" Artero looked surprised. "I haven't seen him for ages."

"What about you my dear?" Lucinda turned to me.

"I live at Tenderden in my aunt's old cottage, but I work in Ambleside."

Lucinda was obviously curious about what work I did but didn't like to ask so I volunteered.

"I work at Charles Aventine's Art Gallery in the town."

Artero looked up abruptly. "Charles Aventine?"

"Yes." I detected something in his voice. "Why, is anything wrong?"

"No, not wrong exactly. Charles used to own a gallery in London but there was some scandal about stolen paintings. I don't know the exact details, but apparently there were some pretty well-known painters exhibiting in the gallery and one night it was broken into and the paintings were taken. Charles didn't really have an alibi as he claimed he was home in bed, but as he wasn't married there was no one to substantiate his story. The paintings were never recovered, but it rather ruined his reputation. I heard he was now in this area."

"Hush," Lucinda said. " That's just gossip. Serina doesn't want to hear about that."

"Aventine seems a good sort. Serina works there most of the week and enjoys it, don't you?" Paul said.

"Yes I do, and he offers a good service for all the local painters."

"Forget I said anything," Artero said gruffly.

"Come on in. It's time for dinner." Lucinda waved us into the dining room.

I had enjoyed meeting Paul's parents, and we left promising to keep in touch.

As we left, Artero shook my hand. "Watch out for Aventine, he may not be what you think he is." He patted Paul on the back. "Now you've got a real girlfriend, you must visit us more often."

Afterwards in the car, Paul said, "Thanks, Serina. Without your prompting I would never have taken the step, but now I'm glad I did. It was good to see them again and they made us both very welcome."

CHAPTER FOURTEEN

Paul and I settled into a comfortable routine. We met every evening, I made a meal for us, we went to bed together, Paul leaving me in the early hours.

Until suddenly one Sunday he said, "I won't be able to see you tomorrow, I have to do something important." He didn't explain, which was strange as we normally talked about everything and shared our most intimate thoughts.

I didn't like to question him, but I was worried, and it began to dawn on me how precious our friendship was to me.

So on Monday morning I felt restless and decided to go on one of my painting trips. I took the car up into the hills heading for the small village of Templeton, which one of the painters told me contained some beautiful old cottages.

I parked the car off the road outside the village and made my way in on foot.

Turning the corner, there in front of me was the warm honey coloured stone of the cottages. These blended with the more austere frontage of the village church next to which was the inevitable pub, the Gregory Arms, looking out on the village green. The village shop stood nearby. I immediately wanted to paint the scene.

I went back to the car, fetched my easel, a canvas, paints and brushes, and set up the easel on the green itself. I settled down to paint. Normally I would make preliminary sketches and then come back another day to paint. However, this scene was too good to miss, the light was perfect. I was so immersed in my work that I didn't notice that I was being watched by a small brown terrier. It only impinged on my consciousness when it came up and nuzzled my foot. It was Jimpy, the dog from the time I'd met Isobel at the Stock Ghyll falls. I stopped painting and stroked its rough fur.

"Hello, Jimpy, where's Isobel?"

At that he bounded off towards one of the cottages and barked at the door. The door opened and Isobel came out. He jumped up to greet her.

She saw me and came over. "Serina, nice to see you again. What are you doing up here?"

It was self-evident what I was doing, but I supposed she was taken by surprise. I was more interested in what she was doing there.

As if sensing the question she said, "I've just come over to see a friend." She looked at my painting. "This is going to be good. You must exhibit it at our next Town Hall meeting." She seemed in a hurry to get away, turned, waved and went back into the cottage followed by an excited Jimpy.

I supposed that visiting a friend was a reason for being in this remote village, however, it was none of my business, so I went back to my painting.

The light was fading, and I decided to stop. *I can finish this back at home.*

I took a last look around trying to photograph the details in my memory. It was then that I noticed an old blue coupe hidden almost out of sight round the corner of one of the cottages. To my surprise, Isobel came out of the cottage followed by Paul Benson, who was carrying a large flat package, Jimpy barking excitedly round his ankles. As they got into Paul's car I hurriedly packed up my easel and paints, ducking back to my car. I was about to set off when they drove past. Had Paul seen me? It seemed not, but in any case, Isobel would have told him I was there.

Most peculiar, I thought. What is Paul doing with Isobel visiting a friend and coming out with what looked like a painting wrapped in paper?

I didn't like mysteries, and it made me realise how closely I was involved with him.

Next day Paul came into the gallery at lunch time. "Can I take you out to dinner tonight? It won't be up to the standard of the dinners you gave me, but do you like Chinese?"

"Yes, I do," I said, as a disastrous memory of me being taken to a Chinese restaurant by a spotty youth in my teens suddenly surfaced in my mind.

"Then I know a good Chinese restaurant in Ambleside."

That evening Paul arrived late. "Sorry about that. I was delayed by a phone call. Are you ready to go?"

"Not yet. I've been pottering about waiting for you instead of thinking about what to wear."

"You look all right to me. Why not come as you are?"

"Men. You've no idea how important it is for us to prepare for a date. Help yourself to a drink while I go and get ready."

I decided on a figure-hugging jersey dress and tied my hair back.

"You look stunning." My Chanel No. 5 wafted over him. "Good enough to hug."

I nestled in his arms for a moment.

He drove us to Ambleside, parked the car and we walked down the main street. It seemed quite natural to hold his hand. I felt a definite tingle.

The restaurant was packed, but we were given a table tucked away in a corner, which suited me very well. I looked around furtively.

"I should explain. This goes back to my teenage days. A spotty teenager took me to our local Chinese restaurant. I can't remember what we talked about but I do remember looking round and finding a waiter skulking behind a potted palm listening to every word we said. Whenever I think of Chinese restaurants, that memory comes to mind."

Paul looked round swiftly. "No potted palms here." He grinned. "I think you're safe."

After looking at the menu, we ordered sweet and sour pork, lemon chicken, beef with orange, and fried rice. The meal arrived and there was a short interval while we shared dishes and ate.

"What happened to the paintings we found in your attic?" he asked.

I clapped my hand to my head. "I'd forgotten all about them. They are still there in the spare room." Then I told him the story about Roy Blinks really being Roger Flatley, the real owner of the paintings. "He asked me if he could leave them with me for now."

"That's a fantastic story," he said. Then suddenly he got up from the table. "I'm sorry, I've just remembered a phone call I promised to make. Won't be a minute, I'd better go outside to do it as I hate people who use their mobile phones in restaurants."

Now what was all that about? I thought, amusing myself by looking at the menu until he came back.

"Sorry about that. I've paid the bill if you're ready to go." His manner was abrupt, not at all like his former loving self.

I expected him to kiss me, but his manner was strange as he drove us back to my house.

When we arrived, I knew that something was very wrong, the front door was hanging open.

Paul helped me out of the car and we both hurried to the door.

"It's been forced open." Paul swung the door back and forth. His manner changed immediately to the loving tone I knew so well. "Look, the lock has been splintered." He pointed at it.

"Can you smell something?" I asked.

Paul sniffed. "Smells like petrol."

I wanted to rush in but Paul held me back.

"No, let me go in first." He went in cautiously and stood for a moment inside the door listening.

As he did so Jed Thompson came out of the kitchen holding a can of petrol in his hand. He was about to pour petrol over the floor. When he saw Paul he dropped the can. Petrol flooded the floor. He took a box of matches from his pocket, but before he could strike a match Paul was upon him. He staggered, knocked Paul out of the way and made for the door, almost knocking me over. As he went, he lit a match.

"If I can't have this house, you shan't either," he shouted and was about to throw the lighted match into the house when I caught his wrist, blew at the match and extinguished it as he jerked free and made off down the path.

Paul put his arm round me as I sagged in the doorway. He looked at the petrol on the floor, picked up the can and put it down outside the door. "Fortunately no damage was done, just a little spillage which we can mop up safely."

"Just a minute." I went in and looked around, then into the dining room and into the kitchen. "Nothing seems to be touched," I said and then with a cry of anguish, "The paintings!"

I rushed upstairs and into the spare room closely followed by Paul.

The paintings were gone.

Chapter Fifteen

For a moment I hesitated, looking everywhere including under the bed as though in some mysterious way they might have moved. I gave a little cry and sat on the bed. "Roger Flatley's paintings have gone, and I told him they would be safe," I sobbed.

"It's obvious Jed Thompson stole the paintings and was going to set the place on fire to cover the theft," Paul said. "It's really a matter for the police. Will you ring them, or shall I?"

"I'll do it, and then we must tell Roger. Will you stay with me? Someone breaking into the house makes me feel unsafe."

"Of course. You also need a locksmith as soon as possible to repair the door."

"I know one in Ambleside. I'll get on to him after I've phoned the police. Look, you make some tea while I'm phoning. You know where everything is and the kettle is on the hob."

I was surprised how fast the police and Alan Barder, my locksmith, responded. Police Constable Kerridge arrived from Ambleside and soon while we were telling him what happened, Alan arrived to repair the damaged door.

"By rights we need to look for fingerprints to try to prove that it was Jed Thompson who took the paintings," Constable Kerridge said. "In any case we should find his fingerprints on the petrol can so we can get him for that. We'll send someone over in the morning to look around."

"I have to go to work in the morning," I said, "but I can leave the key down at the farm if you like."

"Fred Barker's farm? That will be fine, Miss."

Alan finished working on the front door as the constable left.

"There you are. Let's hope I don't have to keep coming to change your locks!' He handed me a new set of keys. "As good as new, if not better. I'll be off now. Send you my invoice in the morning."

"Thank you. I am most grateful that you came so quickly."

He put his coat on. "Got to respond quickly to something like this. Fortunately we don't get many of this sort. It's mainly someone locking themselves out of the house. You would be surprised at how often that happens. "

"Nice person," Paul said as Alan left. "Now what do we do?"

"I must phone Roger," I said.

"There's nothing he can do tonight. Why not leave it until the morning, you look all in."

"I am a bit tired. Perhaps you're right."

Paul put a protective arm round my shoulders. "Will you be all right on your own, or would you like me to stay the night?"

"I will be fine," I said, not really wanting him to go. "There's a new lock on the door, the paintings have gone, and we've cleaned up the petrol so there's no need for you to worry." I looked fondly at him, put my hand to his cheek and kissed him lightly. "Thanks for supporting me."

He held me close for a moment and left abruptly as a welter of emotions stirred in me.

I retired to bed early but soon dropped off to sleep, having confused dreams. In one of them Paul Benson was holding one of the paintings which he threw into the back of his car. He laughed at me, gave me a push and drove off.

I woke up with his name on my lips.

I suddenly remembered his mysterious phone call. Could he have arranged for the paintings to be stolen? No-one else knew about them, and then there was the phone call from the restaurant. Was the call to Jed Thompson?

I was troubled. On the one hand I felt tremendous love for him but on the other it was a strange thing to do. I didn't know what to think. While I was turning this over in my mind, Nancy came with the milk and I explained about Jed Thompson.

Nancy put her hand to her mouth, "I'd have been frightened out of my wits."

"Fortunately Paul Benson was with me. The locksmith and the police were very quick. Can I leave the key with you so that the police can get in if they need to? Take it back to the farm with you."

"Of course you can," Nancy said. "But what a thing to happen. Was anything stolen?"

"Yes, but I've got to leave early today. I'll tell you about it later."

Nancy waited until I was ready to go. I locked the door and handed Nancy the key. "I'll come down to the farm and collect it when I get back."

I drove first to the cottages and knocked on Roger Flatley's door.

When he answered he invited me in. "I was just making breakfast. Would you like some?"

"I can't stop. I'll be late for work but I wanted to tell you something."

I stood by the fireplace, and took a deep breath. "You know the paintings you left with me?"

"Yes, I've been meaning to come and check on them. Perhaps bring them back here."

I felt terrible. "Oh, Roger, they were stolen while I was out with Paul Benson last night."

Roger looked stunned. "Who could have done this? Have you told the police?" he asked.

"We think it was Jed Thompson. He tried to set fire to my house, but let's talk about it later. I have phoned the police, they may come up with something."

"Right," he said briskly. "You get to work, and I'll make contact later."

Chapter Sixteen

I arrived at the gallery and opened up with my key. As soon as I went in I knew something was wrong. A blank wall stared back at me. Panic stricken I looked around and found more blank spaces. I went into the back room and found the window smashed and some of the paintings scattered all over the floor.

I must phone Charles. I picked up the phone but it was dead, the cord pulled out of the wall socket. I took out my mobile phone and dialled.

A sleepy voice answered the phone.

"Charles, the gallery has been broken into and some paintings have been stolen. Can you get over here quickly?"

"I was just having a lie-in this morning." His voice suddenly sounded wide awake. "I'll be over straight away. Have you phoned the police?"

"Not yet. I thought I should phone you first."

"I'll phone them from here. Wait for me at the gallery."

I went back and opened up, hoping that we wouldn't get any visitors.

Charles arrived and almost at the same time a police car drew up and a police sergeant got out.

"Sergeant Hastings, sir. What exactly has happened here?"

"Sergeant, I've just been told that some of my paintings have been stolen. Serina, show Sergeant Hastings what you found."

The broken window and the scattered paintings told their own story and Charles confirmed that a number of paintings were missing.

"I don't know how they knew which were the valuable ones, but it looks like the work of a professional."

"This is quite a coincidence, sir. Constable Kerridge reported to me this morning that Miss Spelton's paintings have also been stolen."

Charles looked across at me. "Your paintings have been stolen as well?"

"It's a long story, Charles. Don't worry about it now. Concentrate on your own paintings."

"Can you give me an inventory?" Sergeant Hastings asked.

"That's no problem," Charles replied. "They are all listed in here." He took a thick, blue, covered book down from the shelf behind his desk. "Although I don't know what the owners of the paintings are going to say about this."

"Do you have insurance?"

"Yes, of course, but the amount of compensation will be nothing like the real value. Serina, you may as well go home, there's nothing for you to do here. We'll shut the gallery and I will have to assess the damage, give details to the Sergeant and notify the owners."

One my way home I began to think about Paul's phone call at the Chinese restaurant. Could it have been to Jed Thompson? And now there was the theft of paintings from the gallery. Was Paul an art thief?

I desperately needed to talk to someone about this, but who could I trust?

Chapter Seventeen

When I got back, Nancy was at the house waiting for me. "Two policemen came. Mum said I was to stay while they were here. They didn't damage anything. They were very nice and didn't make any mess."

"Thanks, Nancy. Tell your mum I'm very grateful, and to you too."

Nancy left the key and skipped off. I was alone with my thoughts.

Of course, Roger Flatley was the person to talk to. The paintings were his, I could talk to him and get his opinion.

I went down to his cottage and knocked on the door but there was no answer. He must have gone out for his walk. I went back to my house and sat down to think, then the obvious solution hit me. Why not ask Paul directly?

I rang him. "Paul, can I come over? There's something I need to talk to you about."

His cheerful voice on the phone said, "Come on over. I'll be pleased to see you so that I can take a break, but aren't you working today?"

"That's what I need to talk to you about. I'll be there as soon as I can."

When I arrived Paul waved a paint brush at me. "What do you think?" he asked, showing me the painting he was working on. It was a close-up picture of the head of a waterfall. "This is where I find my blue stones. I must show it to you." He looked at me. "You're looking very serious, what's the matter?"

"Sit down Paul, I need to talk to you."

He drew up a cane chair for me to sit on and squatted on a stool opposite me. "What's this all about?"

"I don't know where to begin."

"Then begin at the beginning."

"I'll come straight out with it then. You know about my paintings being stolen. Well, now pictures from the gallery have been stolen."

"I didn't know that," he said, staring. "What is going on?"

"I need to know about the phone call you made the other night at the Chinese restaurant."

"I thought something was worrying you. It's nothing to do with paintings. The explanation is quite simple, but I will have to start at the beginning. You know about my disastrous marriage to Carlotta. What I didn't know was that she knew Isobel from the old days. They were both born in the same village. Keeping in touch, Isobel invited Carlotta to stay with her. But Carlotta knew from Isobel that I was in this area and to avoid bumping into me she rented a cottage out at Templedon. Isobel told me she was there and what you saw was me visiting Carlotta with Isobel. I was taking one of my paintings to give to her as a peace offering but she refused it and I came out with it to the car."

I reached out and held his hand. "I'm so relieved. I thought it was something to do with the picture thefts. It's been building up in my mind."

He looked serious. "You don't think that I arranged to steal the paintings?"

"Paul, I'm sorry. I didn't know what to think. Now I feel such a fool. Can you forgive me?"

He squeezed my hand. "Of course, You were the reason I wanted to get my ex-wife off my mind. I was having such a lovely time with you that night when I suddenly remembered that I meant to phone Isobel to tell her to keep Carlotta away from me." He kissed me gently on the cheek.

Charles phoned and said that I needn't come in for a few days as the police were still investigating.

Paul rang, and when he heard I wasn't working, he invited me to go out with him the next day. "I'll show you where I find my blue stones above the waterfall at Windermere."

"I'll make a picnic," I said.

It was a glorious day. Paul was an excellent driver and I relaxed, the wind blowing gently through my hair.

The waterfall above Windemere thundered down, throwing spray in all directions. We parked in the car park alongside the river. I was surprised that there were no other cars.

"Probably a bit early for the tourists. I suggest we leave things in the car for now. I want to show you where I find the blue stones, then we can pick a spot down here for a picnic. Now we have to climb up and go over a bridge at the top of the falls."

We climbed up the rocky path by the side of the falls. Quite a steep climb, and it wasn't an easy path, more of a scramble over boulders, but in the end we reached the top, spray all around us.

Paul pointed to a rickety bridge. "We have to go over that."

I stared at it in alarm. The bridge looked as if it wouldn't support the weight of a person, and the thought occurred to me that one false step and you would find yourself plunging down into the river below. However, I didn't want to appear cowardly. "Fine, I'll follow you across." I trembled as I looked down into the swirling water.

There was a handrail, so very cautiously I stepped on to the bridge with the water thundering below me and inched my way across.

Paul walked across confidently in front of me as he must have done many times before.

When we got to the other side I sat down on a grassy bank. Paul looked concerned and put his arms around me. "Are you all right? It's a bit frightening the first time, but I've done it so often I don't notice it now. If you are all right, I'll show you where I find the blue stones." He took my hand and led me through the trees to a clearing. "This used to be a quarry in the old days, but it isn't working now."

We stopped at what looked like a sheer drop.

"You do take me to some difficult places." I looked down.

"Don't worry, I'll hold on to you." He held my hand tightly, helping me down a path where gorse and bracken grew all around. Even with trousers, the prickles caught at my legs.

"Here we are." We reached not the bottom of the quarry but a bend in the path.

He bent down and took his knife from his pocket poking at an outcrop of rock. He held up a small piece of rock and I could see that it was the same pale blue colour as the one in his workshop. "It needs cleaning up a bit, but it's the same as before. I don't know how far this seam extends but I have enough to last me quite a while."

"Do you get all your rocks like this?" I asked.

"Yes, I'm always exploring the area to find new colours. I haven't been down to the bottom of this waterfall yet, but if you agree we can explore."

I looked at the precipitous slope we were perched on. "Yes, I think I would like to go back."

"Sorry, I was letting my enthusiasm run away with me. Come on."

He helped me up the slope, then held me as we walked over the bridge, which swayed alarmingly.

We picnicked at the bottom of the falls by a small pond which spread out from the river. Paul opened the ground sheet and I unpacked the picnic basket.

Towering above us, the majestic flow of water roared into the river below. A blackbird came to drink at the pool, daintily sipping the water with its beak.

"It doesn't seem frightened," I said.

"I expect it gets used to the tourists."

The bird hopped by us and flew away.

Picnic over, I packed up the remains in the basket and Paul rolled up the ground sheet.

"What do we do now?" I asked.

"I would like to explore," he said.

"Explore where?" I was feeling a bit sleepy with sunshine and wine.

"I can go on my own if you like while you sit in the car?"

"No, I'll come with you."

"This waterfall looks as if it might have a cave behind it. I would like to take a look."

I looked at the forceful water and shook my head, "Even if there were a cave, I don't see how you could get to it."

"I think we can." He stood close to the edge of the falls. "There's a sort of ledge behind the water."

"Be careful," I called, "I don't want you swept into the water." I could hardly hear him over the roar of the falls and next instant he disappeared. I ran towards him.

"I was right." He popped back into sight. "Come on, there is a cave. No, hold on, I've got a torch in the car we shall need if we are going to explore inside."

"I'll get it." I headed back to the car. Looking in the glove box, I found the torch and switched on to test it. It didn't seem very bright. I switched it off, and ran to where he was waiting.

"Come along this ledge. Careful, I won't let you fall."

The water flowed down past us. It was like a curtain. I cowered back as he led me along the ledge and into the dark hole.

"Can I have the torch?" he asked.

I handed it over and he switched it on, its feeble light reflecting back from the glistening cave walls. The cave seemed to go back forever.

"Come on," he said. "Let's explore."

The roar of the water faded as we went further into the cave. Somewhere in the roof something stirred. Shivers went down my spine.

"It's only bats," he said.

I hope not, I thought, imagining them getting entangled in my hair.

"What's this?" He came to a halt in front of a stack of narrow boxes. "I think we've found a smuggler's cave."

"In that case, let's get out of here fast."

"No, I want to see what is being smuggled."

He turned the torch on one of the boxes. "If only I can get this open. Look, it's not really a box, it's some sort of package covered with waterproofing." He took his knife from his pocket and made a slit in the covering. "Hullo, what's this?"

I couldn't see anything as the torch was beginning to fade.

"It's a painting, I can't make out the details, wait a minute." He shone the torch around. "I think all these packages are paintings. What are they doing here?"

"Come on. Let's get out while the going is good, we can talk about it later."

As I spoke the torch winked out and the darkness descended like a blanket. We stood huddled together in the dark. Gradually, as I became accustomed to the dark, I could see a faint light coming from the cave opening. Holding hands we worked our way towards the light.

"I'm sorry about the torch. I keep it in the car but never remember to check it. I'll put new batteries in when we get back."

If we get back, I thought but didn't say so.

The roar of the water intensified, the spray filling the air.

I didn't know how we managed to get back along the ledge but we did. I collapsed onto the passenger seat of the car.

"My hair's wet through," I complained. "Let's go back to my place to get dried out."

Paul shot me an amused look but got into the car and we started back to my cottage.

When we arrived, Paul parked and sat there for a moment looking at me.

"That was quite an adventure. Shall I come in, or do you just want to go in and dry yourself?"

"You'd better come in, if you are as wet as I feel."

"I'm not too bad. I think my trousers are a bit damp, but that's all, my coat held most of it off."

I drew two chairs up in front of the Aga and we sat down. I towelled my hair, then busied myself with the kettle that was soon singing on the hob. We sat there drinking mugs of hot Bovril.

"What are we going to do about the paintings?" I asked.

"We ought to report them to the police. They could be your paintings or the paintings stolen from the gallery."

"Or both. In any case we must tell Charles about them, I will do that first thing in the morning."

CHAPTER EIGHTEEN

Next day I went to the gallery to tell Charles about our find. "There's a cave behind the waterfall above Windemere. We found some paintings in it."

Instead of reacting to that as I expected, Charles put down the painting he was holding and said, "Who's we?"

"Oh, Paul Benson. We went up there for a picnic and discovered this cave."

"A cave? And you say that it contains paintings? Were they wall paintings?"

"No, not wall paintings, these were in waterproof packages in the cave. At least I didn't actually see them myself. there were a number of packages and Paul said he found a painting in one of them."

"Have you told anyone else about this?"

"Not yet, but we thought we ought to tell the police."

"My advice is to forget all about it. It sounds as if some criminal activity is going on, but I wouldn't like you to get involved in anything crooked or illegal. Leave it to me. I will investigate and see what is going on and if necessary contact the police."

"Shouldn't we contact the police anyway?"

"At the moment there's nothing to tell them. I would like to find out exactly what is in that cave before we act."

"All right, Charles. At least I don't have to worry about it, but I hope you know what you are doing. Shall I stay and help you as I'm here?"

"That would be good, thank you." He looked as though he

didn't really want me to stay which puzzled me.

The day passed uneventfully. There was one buyer and three people just looking. Charles had replaced the missing pictures with others from the stockroom.

I was surprised that he didn't seem to make the connection between the packages in the cave with the ones stolen from the gallery, but I reasoned that I wasn't employed to worry about that. I was only too pleased that Charles was providing me with an income.

After work I went back home to tea and cake, did a few household chores, had a long luxurious bath, and then phoned Paul to tell him the news.

"I don't think we should let this go," Paul said. "It's all very well for Charles to say leave it alone. How about coming with me up to the waterfall to see who goes into the cave?"

"I'm game, but the problem is timing. You would have to be up there for quite a long time, and then you might not see anything."

"True, but how about going up to paint the falls. That would keep us up there for some time."

"Good idea. But I have to work during the day and I have a feeling that the thieves won't come in the daylight. Let's take a flask of coffee and something to eat and go up to the falls after dark tomorrow night?"

"All right," he said. "But how do we know they haven't been there tonight?"

"That's a thought. If they are the same thieves, surely they will lie low for a while."

"Good point," he said. "Anyway, let's plan for tomorrow night. We can take some blankets, taking it in turns to watch while the other rests."

I nodded. "Fine. Let's do it."

Next day at the gallery Charles was in a funny, jumpy mood. One minute he would be fussing over a customer and the next he would make some excuse and leave the gallery. I don't know where he went.

The day passed slowly, and when I went to get my lunch sandwich from the local shop, the sky overhead looked black and forbidding. The forecast that morning said there was a possibility of rain.

I thought about our adventure for the evening. I supposed even if it rained we would be snug in the car, but shouldn't we first go into the cave to see if the packages were still there? That was a prospect I wasn't looking forward to. Perhaps I could persuade Paul to do that bit on his own.

I woke from my reverie. My lunch hour came to an end and I needed to deal with a customer as Charles was still out. This was a real customer who wanted to buy a picture of the fells. It made me think of my own painting. It was only on Sundays and Mondays that I could do any painting. Now if I was going to stay up most of the night it would be even harder to find time to paint.

Evening came. Paul picked me up. I'd made coffee and sandwiches as I thought they would be more suitable than biscuits for a long night's vigil.

We arrived at the empty car park below the falls. The moon shone fitfully from between the clouds and although it wasn't raining, the noise of the falls seemed magnified in the darkness. The car park felt eerie. It was then that we encountered our first problem. The car wasn't close enough for us to observe the entrance to the cave.

"We are going to have to take turns to go up closer to the entrance. I'll take the first watch and you can come and relieve me in an hour," Paul said.

"Right. Can you find a suitable place to hide in?"

"No problem, there are lots of bushes up near the base of the falls. I'll pick a spot and show you when you come."

"How will I know if anything happens?"

"I'll hoot like an owl."

"That's what they do in stories." I laughed. "What do we do if there are any real owls about?"

He lightly smacked my wrist. "You have too vivid an imagination. Now synchronise watches, then come in an hour. Here, have this torch, I've brought two this time with new batteries." He gave me one torch and set off into the darkness.

I shivered as he opened the door, then locked the doors and snuggled down into one of the blankets.

I mustn't fall asleep, I thought as I settled down.

The moon shone out from behind the clouds and I could see a figure making its way towards the cave entrance.

I forgot to ask him if we should go into the cave to check, I thought sleepily.

Warm and comfy, I woke up to someone tapping on the window. It was Paul. I unlocked the doors to let him in.

"It's over an hour," he said accusingly. "You fell asleep."

"Sorry, it was just too comfy in this blanket."

"There's no point in you going out for your hour. I haven't been in the cave, but I have a feeling that they won't come tonight. I'll come over tomorrow afternoon and check the cave. We can try again tomorrow."

I looked out at the darkness and felt grateful that I didn't need to hide in the bushes.

Paul took me home and we ate our sandwiches at the kitchen table. Because it was late he left, agreeing that he would pick me up again tomorrow night.

I tumbled into bed and was fast asleep in a moment.

Next day was Sunday, my day off, so I stayed an extra half hour in bed but was roused by a knock on the door. I slipped on a dressing gown and went down to answer it. It was Nancy from the farm. Every morning she brought fresh milk but usually just left it on the doorstep, so I wondered what was wrong.

"Mum sent you some eggs this morning. I didn't like to leave them on the doorstep in case they got broken. Sorry if I disturbed you."

"Thanks Nancy, that's all right. I was just about to make breakfast. Would you like a cup of tea?"

"No, I won't stay, I've got a lot to do at the farm, but thanks anyway."

I watched her hurry down the path. Good neighbours, I thought, and a good neighbourhood apart from Jed Thompson.

I looked out at the dawn breaking over the hills, the rooks sailing by in their daily search for food. I now thought of them as *my rooks,* for as regular as clockwork they flew out in the morning and returned home as a flock in the evening. A sense of wellbeing filled my soul.

The day passed quickly with household chores, and I spent a little time after lunch reading one of my penny dreadfuls. Curiously, though, the story didn't seem as satisfying as it used to. Real life and love with Paul in the Lake District was much more interesting.

I must do some more painting, I thought, I've been lazing the day away. Next week I will be more disciplined.

I made coffee and sandwiches, watched the six o'clock news on television and waited eagerly for Paul to come.

Was the nightly vigil just an excuse to be together, I wondered. It did seem a bit silly to expect that we were going to catch thieves moving their ill-gotten gains at midnight or some unearthly time in the morning.

Paul arrived on time, sounded his horn and I went out clutching my blanket and the basket containing the *midnight feast.*

"I've an idea," he said as I got into the car. "I checked the cave this afternoon and the packages are still there, but I realised that the only way to get them out is through the car park. It's not a good idea for us to park there as we would be seen. I've found a place nearby where we can park the car off the road and be out of sight."

We took it in turns to watch the cave that night, but I found it most unpleasant huddling in a bush for an hour or so. We watched until two in the morning and nothing happened.

"This is silly," I said as we went back and Paul dropped me off. It was a bright moonlight night, shadows danced on the ground as clouds scudded across the sky.

"I won't come in. I agree with you, it is silly to keep going back when nothing happens. Can you make it for lunch tomorrow so that we can discuss what to do next?"

"Monday is usually my day off, but for some reason Charles has asked me to go in. Come to the gallery and pick me up? My lunch hour is one till two."

"I'll be there." He leant forwards and gave me a quick kiss on the cheek.

Next day at the gallery, Charles was quite abrupt. "I've got to go to see Isobel Santir. I'll be back around lunchtime." That was obviously why he wanted me to come in on my day off.

"I have a date for lunch at one o'clock.," I said.

"That's fine. I should be back by then."

But of course he wasn't, and Paul arrived just before one.

"I'm sorry, Paul. Charles said he was going to see Isobel Santir and would be back by one, but he's not, and I can't come out as we don't close for lunch."

"I'll go over to Isobel's house, see if I can dig him out then we can have a late lunch together."

He was gone for quite a while. Charles still hadn't come back.

Paul came back just after one. "Close the gallery and come to lunch, I've got lots to tell you."

"But where's Charles? I suppose if I do lock up he has a key, but I don't know what he will say when he gets back."

"He said he would be back at one o'clock. It's now gone one. He will understand that you have to have some food. Come on."

I put the closed sign on the door, locked up, and we went to the café down the road. It was a good old fashioned tea room, white tablecloths on the tables, two waitresses dressed in frilly aprons.

Paul was excited. "You will never guess what I saw."

"Not until you tell me. Wait until we order."

Order given and with the waitress out of the way he said, "I went to Isobel's house and was about to get out of the car when a Land Rover arrived, and guess who got out of it."

"I can't guess. Who was it?"

"It was a thickset man in a battered old coat. Isobel answered the door to him, and I heard her call him Jed."

Chapter Nineteen

"Jed Thompson," I breathed. "What was he doing there?"

"Could be a perfectly logical explanation. Perhaps he's gone to do some gardening for her, but I don't think so, not with Charles there as well."

"What did you do?" I asked.

"They must have seen my car, so I did the only thing I could think of. I went up to the door and knocked. Isobel's butler answered the door. I made the excuse that I must have left my cigarette case there when we were at the soiree. I asked if it had been found. He took this seriously and assured me there was no sign of it, but if it was found he would let me know. I left hurriedly to get back to you."

"Quick thinking, but won't she wonder why you took so long to ask about it?"

"Hopefully I'm seen as an absentminded person, a painter with time on my hands so it shouldn't look strange."

"I hope not," I said.

I arrived back at the gallery after arranging that we would spend one more night's vigil at the cave. Charles still hadn't come back.

"This is the last time," I said to Paul on the phone. "I think it's a waste of time. The thieves might leave the stuff there for months or move it tomorrow. But all right, just once more."

Charles returned about an hour later. In contrast to his earlier abrupt manner, he now seemed more like his normal self.

Paul and I set out again to the cave that evening. This time it was a full moon with no clouds. Everything was lit by a silvery light. The falls with the water cascading down seemed almost magical.

Paul parked amongst the trees as before and took first watch. He was hardly away ten minutes when he came back.

"It's not time," I protested. He put his finger on his lips.

"Shhh. Come on, something is moving."

We crept along the road and up through the bushes. On the way he pointed to a Land Rover parked in the car park with its back open.

We reached the bushes near the cave entrance and peered out.

"Did you see the car," he said. "It looks like the one Jed Thompson was in when he went to Isobel Santir's."

At that moment a figure appeared, coming along the ledge from the cave carrying a large package.

"It's Jed Thompson," I whispered. "At least, I am sure it is. It's certainly his build, but I can't see his face."

Two other figures appeared from beneath the waterfall carrying smaller packages.

As they reached the car the moon shone fully on their faces.

"It's Isobel and Charles with Jed Thompson," I whispered.

"Hush, they might hear you."

We watched while the three of them repeated their journey carrying packages to the car. Eventually the back of the car was full. Jed closed it up and they all got in and drove off.

Paul turned to me. "What do you think of that?"

"So it was Charles all the time stealing his own paintings and presumably mine as well?"

"We don't know for certain. We think they are the paintings, but we don't have any proof."

"Let's get some. Can we follow them?"

"Good thought. Come on back to the car. We should be

able to pick up their trail. The road they took leads up to Langdale Pike."

We stumbled through the undergrowth back to the car. Paul put the sidelights on.

"It's bright enough to see the road and I don't want them to know we are following."

He drove carefully. The moonlight flooded the road with light, trees loomed out of the darkness casting shadows across the road. It took all his attention with just the sidelights on.

Fortunately the lights on the Land Rover were full up and it was possible to see them in the distance.

"Where are they going?" I asked.

"Certainly not back to Windermere. This road heads up into the hills. I wonder what they are up to?"

We soon found out. The Land Rover pulled off onto a rough track near a large house set in grounds surrounded by a high wall. The car drove up to the gates, which were opened as they drove towards them and closed immediately afterwards.

Paul brought the car to an abrupt halt, backing it up under the cover of trees.

He switched the engine off and cut the side lights. "I don't think they heard us."

You hope, I thought.

"What do we do now?" I asked.

"Short of climbing over the wall, there's not much we can do,"

We got out of the car and crept towards the wall.

The wind was cool. I shivered, drawing my coat closer. Somewhere nearby there was the sound of a night bird.

Paul helped me up onto his shoulders so that I could look over the wall.

I called down softly. "There's a helicopter on the lawn and their car is drawn up to it."

"Don't be long," Paul called back. "I can't bear your weight for much longer."

As I watched, figures got out of the Land Rover, opened the back doors carrying packages from the car to the helicopter. It didn't take long. There was a whirring noise as the rotor blades began to revolve. I collapsed on to Paul as the helicopter took off. We dived into the bushes.

The Land Rover came out of the gates turning onto the road towards Windemere while the helicopter gained height and disappeared up into the hills.

Now the coast was clear, we emerged from the bushes and stood for a moment in the moonlight.

"We can't follow the helicopter and presumably Charles and the others have gone home, so there's not much we can do tonight."

"We could climb over and see who is in the house."

"You're an adventurous young lady, but I think that's enough for tonight."

As he spoke there was a rustle in the bushes on the opposite side and a figure emerged carrying what looked like a gun.

I grabbed Paul's hand and turned to run. *They must have left someone on guard.*

"Hold on a minute," someone called.

I hesitated, I thought I knew the voice.

The figure came up to us and turned into Roger Flatley, holding not a gun but a stout stick.

Paul turned. "Who is this?"

"It's Roger, my neighbour, the real owner of the paintings from my house, but what are you doing up here?"

"Probably like you—I'm tracking picture thieves." He came towards us over the rough ground.

We stood there, three figures outlined in the moonlight.

"I think we ought to join forces," he said. "I've been watching this house for some time. They use it as a distribution point for the stolen paintings. I can see I will have to tell you all about it, but not tonight, it's too late. How about a meeting tomorrow? Serina knows a bit about me, and I should tell you both a bit more."

Paul said, "Right. Where shall we meet?"

"Why not come for a meal at my place?" I said.

We agreed to meet the next day at seven in the evening.

Paul drove me back, took me in his arms and kissed me gently.

"How are you going to face Charles, knowing what you know?"

"The same thought occurred to me. The answer is I don't know but will let you know tomorrow."

I seemed to be getting into the habit of getting back late and falling into bed, but this time before retiring I made myself a cup of hot chocolate and took it up with me.

Sitting up in bed with the comforting warmth and the aroma of chocolate I reviewed the situation. How would I feel facing Charles in the morning knowing that he was a thief? And how was Isobel Santir involved? Jed Thompson was easier to understand, as he was an obvious bad lot to start with.

I drank my warm drink and settled down to sleep. The memory of Paul's kiss came back to me. With that thought in mind I fell asleep.

Next morning I still didn't know how to react to Charles but it was a work day so I went to the gallery.

Charles was there already and was his usual self, greeting me warmly and immediately setting me to work cataloguing some paintings. When he spoke to me, I answered in monosyllables and tried to avoid looking at him. I realised that he would spot that something was wrong but couldn't help it. I was relieved when he said he was going out and I guessed that he was off to see Isobel again. He said he would be away for the rest of the day and would I lock up.

The day dragged on. I wished I was having lunch with Paul but contented myself with a sandwich. There were only two visitors and they just browsed, buying nothing.

I sat looking at Charles' desk, which was a grand affair of oak and walnut and it was always untidy. It sat in an alcove at the back. I wondered if something in it might give us a clue to what Charles was up to. I riffled through the papers on top, but there were only invoices and bills that seemed to refer to legitimate deals. I tried the drawers, but they were all locked and I certainly wasn't going to prise them open.

After locking up the gallery I went to the local supermarket and bought fillet steak, potatoes, and broccoli for the main meal, a bottle of red wine, and some nice ripe peaches for afters with cheese biscuits and olives for nibbles.

Paul and Roger were due at seven, so when I got back I riddled the Aga, set the table and got to work.

I was looking forward to having guests.

Roger arrived early but was quite happy to sit in the kitchen with a whisky while I finished cooking.

Paul arrived on time bringing with him a bottle of champagne. "I thought we might as well make the evening an occasion as well as talk business."

"Business after dinner," I said. "So it's champagne and nibbles first, then the meal."

It was a friendly atmosphere. Paul and Roger hit it off well together and the meal was a success.

After dinner, relaxing by the fire, Roger said, "Thank you for a marvellous meal, now I suppose I must sing for my supper."

"Yes please," Paul said. "What's it all about?"

Roger turned to me. "I've told you about losing my memory. You helped me get it back with the letters your aunt kept, but what neither of you know is that I am not just in this area by chance. I work for the PPB, the Preservation of Paintings in Britain. We're a private organisation funded by the Arts Council and work closely with the police and other authorities. We have been concerned for some time that valuable paintings are being stolen from museums and art galleries across the country and shipped abroad."

"I thought we were just dealing with your stolen paintings and a local theft from Charles' Gallery."

"Far from it. We don't know who the leader is, but the gang has a network of contacts across the country, and several of our leads follow a trail leading back to this area. Also, Dover is the nearest port to France, so the thieves take the paintings there and then sell them illegally somewhere in Europe."

"If you know so much, why haven't you been able to catch them?"

"It's only recently we managed to get a lead to the Lake District. All we knew was that there were several distribution points across the country. We intercepted a shipment at Dover and one of the men confessed that the main distribution point was in the Lake District. So here I am."

"I don't understand why you took a cottage at Tenderden?" Paul said.

"It was pure chance. As I told Serina, I felt a strange affinity to the place and thought it would be good to explore the area from here. Then I came across Jed Thompson, saw packages going in and out of his cottage, followed him to the cave, and knew I was onto a winner."

"I see," Paul said thoughtfully. "So you knew about the cave?"

"Yes, they have used it on several occasions, and the rendezvous point where we met. I've been in the house they use. It's empty and in such a desolate spot I doubt if anyone would want to live there, but it makes a useful distribution point. I need all the help I can get. That's why I'm telling you this. I'm on my own up here, so to have two other people working with me would be great."

"What is there to do?" I asked. "The paintings have gone, so surely there won't be any activity for a while."

"We think there is another shipment coming soon. Serina, could you watch what Charles puts into his stock room and report back to me?"

"I'm not sure I like that," Paul said. "Won't Serina be in danger if Charles finds her snooping around?"

"I'll be careful." I put my hand on his arm. "In any case I shall be keeping in touch with both of you."

The evening drew to a close. Paul offered to stay and help me wash up but I was too tired and said that Nancy would be coming in the morning and would help. They both left together after making sure we took each other's phone numbers, promising to keep in touch.

CHAPTER TWENTY

Next morning Nancy arrived with the milk and then, as before, came in to clean and tidy the house. I apologised for all the dirty dishes and offered to help.

"It's no problem," she said. "I enjoy helping and you have to go out."

I was late leaving as I did help Nancy with the washing up. I made my way down to Ambleside. I arrived at the gallery only to find instead of the usual *closed* notice, a larger notice which read *The Gallery is closed until further notice.* Charles had obviously been in early and it looked, from the notice, as though he wasn't coming back.

I unlocked the door with my key and slid in, closing the door behind me. I went first to the stock room and found it empty except for one or two canvases that I recognised as being from local artists. Next I went to his desk. All the drawers were unlocked and empty. I locked the gallery up and drove over to Paul's workshop.

"Charles has done a bunk, ' I said, when I arrived. "He's cleared out everything and shut the gallery for good."

"Something or someone must have put the wind up him. I wonder what it was?"

"Don't forget we saw Isobel with him last night. I wonder if she has gone as well?"

"We can soon find out. Let's go over to her house. If she is still there, Charles won't be far away."

We took Paul's car and drove to Isobel's house.

"Best if we park outside and walk up to the house," Paul

said.

He parked the car a little way down the road from the house, and we walked self-consciously up the drive. There were two cars parked in front of the house. One I recognised as Charles' car and the other was the Land Rover they had used for transporting the paintings.

"They are all here," I whispered. "What do we do now?"

"Well, we can't just walk in and accuse them. We ought to call the police." Paul pulled me back into the shrubbery.

We ought to have contacted Roger or gone straight to the police, but we didn't.

We crept round the house to the French windows of the room where Isobel held her parties. The French window was ajar.

"Even better," Paul whispered. "Take a look, and if nobody is around, we can get into the house."

I sidled up to the window and looked inside. "Come on, there's no-one there."

Once inside we could hear voices coming from the next room.

"Can you hear what they are saying?" I asked.

He crept up to the door and put his ear close to the woodwork. "They're saying something about Venice," he whispered back. "Hang on."

Suddenly the voices got louder and we heard Isobel say, "Just a minute, I'll go and get it."

The door opened abruptly and Paul almost fell into her arms. I stepped back in alarm.

"What's this?" she cried.

Paul quickly recovered, "Ah, Isobel we were just coming to see you about arrangements for the next artist's meeting. We heard voices and didn't like to disturb you."

"Nice try but there isn't going to be a next meeting."

Charles, accompanied by Jed Thompson, emerged from behind Isobel.

Charles took in the situation at a glance. "Get them, Jed."

Jed moved menacingly towards us.

I moved away from Paul and took hold of a slim vase from a nearby table.

"Put that down, it's valuable." Isobel threw herself at me.

The thought ran through my mind that although she was old, she was still quite supple.

I was fully occupied with Isobel but could see Paul grappling with Jed. Pushing Isobel away I got behind Jed and brought the vase down on the back of his head.

It shattered. Jed staggered back and released Paul.

"Come on Paul, let's make a run for it." I grabbed his hand and pulled him towards the French window.

"Not so fast." Charles pulled out a revolver. "I won't hesitate to use this. Come back and sit down. Jed, tie them up. You'll find rope in the shed." He shoved us roughly into the dining room and made us sit down. "Now what have you both been up to?"

"I don't know what you are talking about," Paul said. "We walk in to talk to Isobel, you attack us and treat us like criminals."

Charles smiled grimly. "Perhaps, or perhaps you overheard us talking. In any event we can't risk it. You are going to have to stay here while we make our departure. Ah, Jed, tie them up."

Jed tied us to the chairs we were sitting on. He used too much rope on me, winding it round and round.

I tried an experimental wriggle and felt the rope slacken while he was occupied in tying Paul up.

Charles put the revolver away and called Isobel. "Let's get going."

They left the room and there were sounds of two cars starting up, the noise fading into the distance.

Paul looked across at me. "When we get free from this, I shall give you the biggest hug I can manage."

"That might be sooner than you think. I can feel the ropes loosening."

I wriggled my bonds and managed to get a hand loose. Paul was trying the same thing but without much success. I found the main knot on the rope and by working at it I was able to untie myself. I went over to Paul and untied him. We stood for a moment in each other's arms.

Paul kissed me tenderly. "It's too late to go after them now. Let's go and find Roger."

As we reached the cottages a thought occurred to me. "I wonder if Jed told his wife where he was going?"

"Good thought. Let's go to see her before we get to Roger."

I knocked on the door of Jed's cottage and a neatly dressed woman in a floral apron answered the door.

"I'm Serina Spelton, a near neighbour of yours. We wanted to get in touch with Jed. Do you know when he will be back?"

She looked nervously at us. "I don't rightly know." She clutched at her apron. "He went out this morning without saying a word."

"Thank you Mrs Thompson. It is Mrs Thompson?"

"That's right, I'm Hilda Thompson. What has my Jed been up to now? Are you the lady up at Miss Renault's old house? Won't you come in for a minute?"

"Thank you, but we must get on."

She looked disappointed.

She closed the door and I looked at Paul. "That's a worried wife. I wonder if she knows what Jed is up to?"

"It doesn't look like it, but let's get to Roger." He knocked at Roger's front door.

Roger opened it immediately.

We went in and Paul explained how we had been tied up while Charles, Isobel and Jed left.

"They were pretty desperate, to pull a gun on you," Roger said in alarm.

"Something must have gone wrong with their plans, as Isobel wouldn't abandon her house lightly."

"Do you think they might come back?" I asked.

"I don't think so," Paul said. "Since Charles was waving a revolver about—he wouldn't have done that if they planned to return."

"You're probably right," Roger said. "So now we have them on the run but we are no further forwards, although you did hear them mention Venice. I must get in touch with my boss in London."

As Paul and I were about to leave, a Land Rover drew up outside the cottages. It was Jed. He got out of the car and went into his own cottage without seeing us. He seemed in a hurry.

I turned to Roger. "What do we do now?"

"Back in the cottage. We'll call the police, and they can get him."

The police car had to come from Windermere. I kept looking out of the window thinking that Jed would take off before they came, but fortunately he didn't.

The police car arrived and Sergeant Hastings got out. Roger greeted him. They obviously knew each other.

"What's this all about?" he asked.

"It's the picture thieves. Jed Thompson is one of them and at the moment he is in his cottage."

Sergeant Hastings, a rather stout man, was just saying, "We know all about Jed," when Jed shot out of his front door, into his car and was away, driving like a madman.

Sergeant Hastings quickly eased himself back into his car, switched on the siren and took off after him leaving the three of us looking at each other.

"Why did he come back?" Paul asked.

"Perhaps he wanted to say goodbye to his wife."

"A cold-hearted devil like that. More likely he needed to pick up some money before he scarpered."

"I'm sure Hastings will do his best to catch him, but what about the other two? I have an idea, come back inside." Roger motioned us in. "I told you I thought there was another shipment due. I can't see Aventine or Isobel passing that up. I think we should go back up to the cave to see if there's anything there. If there is, then we can set a trap."

We all piled into Paul's car and set off up to the waterfall.

It was beginning to get dark when we arrived, and there were no cars in the car park.

Paul said, "Come on, Roger. Let's take a look in the cave, there might be something there. Serina, no need for you to come, we shan't be long."

They took torches and made off in the direction of the falls. The noise of the water made me drowsy.

I woke up with a start as the door was jerked open and I was pulled out.

Charles Aventine held me in his grip. He handled me roughly. "Where are your little playmates? In the cave I suppose – well they won't find much there."

He called back to Isobel, who was driving their car. "We'll have to leave the rest of the stuff, they're onto us, but we can keep this one. We might need a hostage."

He lifted me bodily and threw me into the back of their car. They set off in the direction of Windermere.

I lay sprawled on the seat. No-one was restraining me, but the car was going too fast on the winding roads for me to open the door and jump out.

We arrived at the pier on Windermere lake.

"Come on." Charles wrenched me out of the car, down a

flight of wooden steps, and into a cabin cruiser.

I shivered. The night was cold, and I was wearing only light clothes. The boat set off across the lake. I sat huddled in the bow, regaining my strength and watching the ripples on the water.

The boat sped on towards the centre of the lake.

Isobel bent over me. "Are you all right?"

I looked up. "No, I'm not. I grabbed Isobel's arm, pushing her against the side of the boat.

"What's going on?" Charles came out of the cabin.

Isobel tried to grab me, but I twisted out of her grip.

I hesitated for a moment as she made a grab at me ,then I jumped over the side of the boat and into the water. I swam strongly away from the boat.

I heard Isobel yell, "Get after her."

Chapter Twenty-One

I dived down under the water. When I surfaced the boat had sped away. I struck out for the shore and stood dripping wet, shivering and wondering what to do next.

A man was walking along the shore with his dog. He saw me and stopped. "You're wet through, my dear. Did you fall in?"

My teeth were chattering. "Not exactly. Can you get me to a phone? I don't think my mobile will work after all that water. "

"I think you need more than a phone. My place is just along the shore. Come with me. My wife will be able to fit you up with some dry clothes and yes, we do have a phone." The man took off his coat and put it over my shoulders.

"Thank you," I said, shivering.

He whistled to his dog, a golden retriever, and quickly led me to a group of houses next to a boat yard.

"Come in." He opened the door of the first house.

I entered a bit hesitantly and stood dripping on the door mat. The dog brushed past me and bounded into the hallway.

"Daisy," the man called, "We need your help."

His wife came out of the kitchen, took one look and led me into the warmth of the kitchen.

"Fred, get me a large white towel from the airing cupboard and then make yourself scarce." She closed the kitchen door. "You poor dear, let's get you dry and then we can sort this out." Daisy was a comfortable motherly woman.

There was a knock at the kitchen door. Daisy opened it,

took the offered towel and then shut the door firmly. "Off with your clothes now. Dry yourself with this towel then we'll run a bath for you. That should warm you up."

Some time later, clothed in one of Daisy's dressing gowns I came down into the living room where a lively fire was glowing and dancing in the hearth.

Daisy and Fred were sitting in front of it, drinks in their hands.

Fred got up. "Sit here. I'll get you a drink. What would you like, we have most things."

"That's kind of you, but I must get to a phone."

"Sit for a minute and then you can phone. How about a gin and tonic?"

"That would be fine," I said. "I expect you are wondering what this is all about?"

"Well, you don't look as though you were trying to do away with yourself, so what happened?"

I accepted the drink. "Can I leave explanations for a minute? I must phone my friends to let them know I'm safe."

"Of course, my dear. Fred, show her the phone," Daisy said.

Fred took me into the hall. "I'll leave you to it. Do you know the number?"

"No, but I can get it from Directory Enquiries."

I tried Paul's number first but there was no reply. Perhaps they were still on the road or had gone to Roger's place.

My next call was successful, they were at Roger's place.

Roger answered the phone. "Serina, where are you? Are you safe? We were so worried when you disappeared from the car."

"I'm all right. I don't know where I am at present but I'm safe. Is Paul with you?"

"I'm here." Paul came on the phone. "What happened? We

came back for you, but you weren't there."

"Charles and Isobel captured me. I was taken on their boat but managed to jump overboard. I've been rescued by a kind couple."

"Tell us where you are and I'll come and pick you up."

"Don't worry about that for the moment, you need to get the police after Charles and Isobel."

"Where were they going?"

"I don't know exactly, but they were heading up Lake Windermere to the other side."

"OK, give me your phone number and I'll ring you back after we have contacted the police. Then we can pick you up."

Fred had come back and was standing a little way from me. He came forward. "The phone number is zero four six five two nine five four and the address is The Willows, Boat Yard Road."

I relayed it to Paul, replaced the phone and went back into the warmth of the living room.

Fred drew up another chair to the fire. "Now, sit down and tell us all about it. Let me introduce ourselves properly. We are Fred and Daisy Bantler."

I sat in the chair. "I'm Serina Spelton, and I'm sorry to put you to all this trouble."

"No trouble at all." Daisy smiled. "We often rescue damsels in distress, don't we Fred?"

Fred was a short, dark-haired man of about forty. "We haven't done it for a while, but what happened?"

"It's a long story, but briefly I was being held prisoner on a boat, managed to jump overboard and swim ashore. That was when you rescued me."

Daisy got up. "You poor dear, thank goodness Fred was there to help you. Now we were just about to eat. Would you like to join us? You must be hungry."

"Yes, I am. But is it all right if I join you in this?" I indicated the dressing gown.

"That will be fine. I've put your clothes to dry in front of the range in the kitchen. Windermere water isn't the best thing for them, but I can lend you some clothes to go home in."

"My friends said they would call your number and come to pick me up."

"Not until you have some food inside you. Come on into the dining room."

The dining room was L-shaped, the table a good old fashioned leaf table set for two people.

Daisy bustled out to get another place setting. "Sit down while I go and get the food."

Fred sat looking at me. "You seem to be having a lot of adventures."

"You don't know the half of it. We've been involved with picture thieves, a cave under a waterfall and . . ."

Daisy came back into the room. "Your friend called. Do you want to speak to him? I've left the phone for you."

I went into the hall and picked up the phone.

It was Paul, who said, "We'll come for you."

"Yes, thanks. Don't rush, I've got to get some clothes on."

"That sounds bad." I could almost see Paul grinning. "See you soon."

I replaced the receiver and went back into the dining room.

After eating and sitting for a while, Daisy said, "Come on up to the bedroom. You need some clothes. Mine will be a little loose on you." She patted her ample figure. "They will at least cover you. Bring them back when you can."

Dressed in Daisy's blouse, jumper and skirt I made my way back downstairs.

"I can't thank you enough. Rescuing a perfect stranger."

"Don't mention it, my dear. Only glad we could help. I've

put your clothes in this bag. They're pretty well dry but you need to get them cleaned."

"I really am grateful. I will try to bring your things back as soon as I can."

"You can tell us the rest of the story when you come. We don't get much excitement. Come to tea soon," Daisy said.

A car drew up outside and honked its horn.

"That will be Paul. Goodbye, and thank you for everything."

I got in the car, sitting by Paul, waving to them as the car drew away.

I turned to Paul. "Have they caught them?"

"Not yet, as far as we know. They sent a police launch after them but, it was too late. The boat was found abandoned on the other side of the lake. But how about you? Are you all right?"

"I'm fine, Fred and Daisy were very kind to me. Nice people. I'm wearing Daisy's clothes, as mine were wet through from the water. They are in this bag." I plonked it on the floor at the back. "Where's Roger, by the way?"

"He went on the police launch but he's probably back at his cottage by now. I told him I would take you there."

Roger was back at the cottage and embraced me as we came in. "Thank goodness you are all right. Do you want some tea?"

"I've just eaten, but how about you two?"

"We're fine," they said.

"We need to plan." Paul sat down. "I know the police will be after Charles and Isobel, but I think we should do something ourselves."

"It's getting late. What can we do?"

"I think they will be heading for the rendezvous point. That old house we saw. They probably contacted the helicopter to pick them up. That's where they met the helicopter last time.

Let's go." Paul got up and walked to the door.

"Wait. I've got something we can use to get over the wall when we get there." Roger went into the back room and brought out a flexible scaling ladder with hooks at one end.

"Very useful. You seem to be equipped for all emergencies."

Paul turned to me. "Sorry I wasn't thinking. Let us handle this. Stay here, you must be absolutely beat."

I sat up straight in my chair. "Just you try to leave me out. I'm coming with you."

"At least put this coat on." Roger handed me an old army great coat.

"I must look like a bag lady in this." I shrugged into the coat. "Come on, let's go."

We piled into Paul's car. I sat in the back. "You won't mind if I fall asleep." I snuggled down into the warm coat.

The next thing I knew, the car pulled up with a jolt outside the wall of the house where the helicopter was last seen.

Roger got out and picked up the ladder from the boot. He threw the ladder up onto the wall. "I'll go over. You two wait."

He took a torch, scrambled up and disappeared into the darkness. After what seemed an age he reappeared and got into the car. "They have been here. Their car is still there but the grass on the lawn is freshly flattened so we can assume the helicopter picked them up and is gone."

"What do we do now?"

"Not much we can do," Roger said. "I think I should report to my boss in London and ask for further orders. I'll mention the help the two of you have given me and will make contact again tomorrow."

We made our way back. Paul dropped Roger and me at our cottages before he went back to John Turner's farm.

Chapter Twenty-Two

Next day I couldn't settle on anything. The day seemed to drag. I spoke to Paul on the phone, but no word from Roger until late afternoon.

"I've spoken to my boss, Major Jackson, in London," he said. "I told him the whole story including the two of you. I'm phoning Paul after I get off the phone with you. The Major wants us all to go to London tomorrow. He seems to have some plan in mind that would involve the three of us. Are you game to come?"

I let the phone dangle in my fingers for a moment, then I decided. "Yes of course, assuming Paul agrees. It will be an adventure."

"Good for you, I'll phone him now."

I put the phone down. *What was I letting myself in for*?

A few minutes later the phone rang again. It was Roger.

"Paul says yes. You can leave everything to me. Pack a case for say, three days. I'll sort out the travel arrangements and find somewhere for us to stay in London. Phone you both later to tell you which train we're catching at Windermere. We can fix the local taxi to take us."

It was like a dream. Roger called to say that the taxi would call for me at ten o'clock the next morning.

Paul called to say that he would be coming over early and would it be all right if he left his car with me.

I didn't sleep very well, and then it was morning. I was still packing when Paul arrived.

Roger arrived at ten o'clock in the taxi with Sid Chapman

grinning at the wheel.

The train was ten minutes late. We were able to get lunch in the restaurant car before we arrived at Euston station in London.

From the train we went by taxi directly to a building on the Embankment.

We were taken upstairs by an orderly along a long corridor painted in battleship grey and brown to a door marked PPB. The orderly knocked and a loud military voice called, "Come in."

We stood in front of a mahogany desk covered in papers. The large red-headed figure behind the desk looked up as we entered. "Ah, Blinks, or should I call you Roger Flatley now? Sit yourselves down over there."

Major Jackson came round the side of the desk, shook hands with each of us, and indicated the easy chairs by the fireplace. "You seem to have collected quite a band of helpers." He looked thoughtfully at Paul and me. "Are you game to help us catch these crooks?"

"What do you want us to do?" Roger asked.

"It means a trip to Venice," Major Jackson said.

At that Paul looked up. "When we were in Isobel's house, I heard them talking about Venice."

Major Jackson turned to him. "Yes, we believe the centre of operations is in Venice, although we don't know exactly where. Your task, should you care to accept it, is to go to Venice as tourists, make contact with our man out there and report anything you find."

"I've always wanted to go to Venice," I said. "One of my painter friends said it was her ambition to paint in a garret in Venice."

"Well now you get your chance." Major Jackson smiled. "But first I need all three of you to take a look at photographs of the paintings we know to have been stolen."

He pressed a button on an intercom. "Send Travers in, will you?"

He explained. "Bertha Travers will take you down to our viewing room where she will show you what we have. Ah, Travers."

A large well-built woman in an army uniform came into the room, saluted, and stood waiting for orders.

Major Jackson introduced her. As we were about to follow her out, Major Jackson called Roy back. "Hang on a minute, I need to discuss some final details with you."

Roy turned to us. "Go on down. I'll join you in a minute. I know my way."

We followed Bertha down several flights of stairs to an underground room fitted out as a small cinema.

As we went down I whispered to Paul, "I thought Roger said this was a private organisation? It seems more like a military one."

Bertha heard me. "You're right, my dear. We are all ex-military, but sit yourselves down." She waved at the comfortable chairs. "I'll get the pictures up and give you a running commentary."

She slid out of sight behind a small projection booth. The room lights went down, the first picture came up on the screen and her voice, low and almost masculine, came over the speakers.

"This one is a Degas. It was stolen last year from Roxley Manor in Kent. It has never been recovered, and we believe it has made its way to Venice."

Although the room was obviously air conditioned, I felt myself getting drowsy as picture followed picture on the screen while Bertha's voice droned on.

Just as I felt myself nodding off, Roy came into the room, sliding into one of the chairs. "Everything's fixed. I'll tell you about it afterwards."

The procession of pictures continued until at last it stopped and Bertha turned the main lights on.

"That's the lot." She came out of the booth. "Mr Flatley, I'll show you the ones that you missed later. Now I expect you need a cup of tea, I know I do. These sessions exhaust me. Come on, I'll take you to the canteen."

After the darkness of the projection room the canteen was light and airy.

I sipped the welcome tea as Roger explained the arrangements that were being made. "I won't be travelling with you. You are a young couple on holiday. I shall meet you in Venice. All you have to do is keep your eyes open and report anything you find to me. You are staying in London tonight in a hotel near City airport. You will find your plane tickets and final details in your rooms. Don't worry," he said, laughing. "We've booked you into separate rooms."

Little did he know!

After that, all went smoothly. Air tickets and details of the hotel in Venice, together with the rendezvous, were all in sealed envelopes in our rooms.

We flew from City airport, arriving at Marco Polo airport, Venice by lunchtime.

"Both airports are so near the water." As I looked out, I thought the plane narrowly missed dropping into the water.

We came out into the departures area, where an attractive woman in a blue uniform waved a board on which was written our names.

We went up to her and she immediately ushered us into a waiting boat. The boatman, dressed in striped jersey and cap, introduced himself as Marco.

The boat sped through the water, throwing up spray which glinted in the sunlight. Other boats passed going in the opposite direction, separated from us by rows of wooden poles marking the way.

As we came to the Grand Canal, I marvelled at the sight of the magnificent buildings clustered along the front.

Marco pointed at one. "That is your hotel." He expertly brought the boat round in a wide circle, jumping out and tying up at the landing stage as a uniformed porter came out to greet us. We waved goodbye to Marco and followed the porter into the hotel's impressive entrance.

I stood overwhelmed for a moment by the palatial splendour. Two marble pillars dwarfed the reception desk.

A woman in a uniform similar to the porter's greeted us in English. "I'm sorry there is no lift. The porter will take your cases up to your room on the first floor."

He took us along a wide corridor carpeted in what seemed to be purple velvet, stopping at the third door on the left, which he threw open.

"This is for the Signorina." He put Paul's case down and took mine into the room.

Paul followed me in, curious to see what the room was like.

The porter immediately shooed him out. "Your room is along the corridor," he said.

Paul followed him out.

I stood transfixed. My room was enormous. On the left hand side a large canopied double bed stood guarded by two golden lions. On the right-hand side was a sitting area resplendent with deeply upholstered chairs in purple velvet.

I stood for a moment wondering where the bathroom was. *I'm surprised he didn't show me.*

As I stood there, Paul knocked at the door and came in.

He looked at the opulent surroundings. "My room is the same. I dread to think what Major Jackson is paying, but he's certainly doing this properly."

"I was just wondering where the bathroom was."

"It's behind that door," he said, indicating a door behind

the sitting area. "Do you need it?"

"No, I'll explore later. What do we do next?"

"I think lunch would be a good idea, then a stroll round outside to get our bearings."

We went back down to the front hall, and on enquiring about lunch, we were shown into a room adjoining the large dining room where small tables were set out for lunch. There were a number of couples in the room, the sound of gaiety, the room was light and airy.

I felt my spirits lift. I was in a city full of art and painters. I felt comfortable but reminded myself that we were on a mission to find out all we could about the stolen paintings. It was hard to concentrate on that when everything seemed so normal.

"Are you hungry?" Paul asked. "I am. What about a smoked salmon sandwich and a glass of wine?"

"That sounds just the thing."

Paul ordered the sandwiches and two glasses of Pinot Grigio.

As we drank our wine, Paul leant back in his seat. "I'm not sure if you want to go for a stroll? You might prefer for us to have a rest in your room."

I looked at his innocent face. "You want us to have a snooze in my room?"

He grinned. "Well, perhaps not exactly a snooze."

A thrill ran through my body.

Chapter Twenty-Three

I grabbed his hand as he put his glass down on the table and practically dragged him back to my room.

"Wait, wait." He stood in the doorway looking embarrassed. "I need to get something from my room."

I guessed what it was and released his hand. "Come as quickly as you can. I'll leave the door unlocked."

He bounded off and I went into my room, quickly stripped my clothes off, and lay naked on the bed. It seemed only seconds before he was in the room. He closed the door and turned the key in the lock, then coming over to me, he stood for a moment admiring my body. As he bent over to kiss me I grabbed him and he collapsed onto the bed. I quickly unbuttoned his shirt. He struggled out of it, slid to the edge of the bed, kicked off his shoes, stepped out of his slacks and slid his briefs down. I could see that he was sheathed and ready. I put my arms round him and pulled him back onto the bed, opening my legs to him.

He turned and our naked bodies entwined. I felt my heart leap as he thrust into me, I felt the warmth of his body, the kisses, the caresses, the wonderfulness of being together. His thrusts became more urgent and we came together in a wonderful moment.

I felt the joy of being totally as one that evening, our mission almost forgotten.

That night we slept together in my big bed, making gentle love again before falling asleep. I must have dreamt but could remember nothing when I woke except the warmth of Paul's body next to mine.

He went to his own room to wash and dress. He said he would meet me downstairs in the breakfast room.

I got there first and was shown to a corner table. He came in, saw me and sat next to me.

"I'm looking forward to exploring this morning, St Mark's Square isn't far from this hotel is it?" I said excitedly.

As our breakfast arrived, Paul looked up at the waiter. "How do we find St Mark's Square?"

"It is easy, Signor. Turn right out of the hotel and it is about a five-minute walk along the canal."

Paul nodded. "Thank you." He raised his glass of orange juice as though it was champagne. "To us, it's not only an adventure, it's a holiday."

And it was like a holiday. After breakfast we strolled down the road alongside the Grand Canal and were immediately surrounded by a crowd of tourists following a guide holding a folded umbrella above her head.

I noticed that the tourists were laughing, talking and seeming not to take any notice of the beauty around them. The sun glinting on the waters of the canal, rows of gondolas gently swayed, moored at a landing stage. A vaporetto, water bus, painted red, green and black, moving slowly through the water.

Paul took my hand. "Let's get away from the crowd."

He hurried me past the stout woman holding the umbrella and on towards St Mark's Square.

We arrived at the square, a vast open area filled with crowds and crowds of people. A number of them were standing round a clock tower looking up at it.

I could see people of many nations filling the square. Among them were sellers of ice cream, postcards, ribbons and souvenirs. A photographer was snapping pictures of happy couples.

Paul was still holding my hand. "What do you think of it?" he asked.

"It's breath-taking. What are all those people doing looking up at the clock?"

"Come and see." Paul led me over to join the crowd. As we looked, there was a creak of ancient machinery and ornate figures standing by the clock raising their hammers, striking the hours on a small bell.

The crowd turned away as the last stroke of the bell died away.

Turning, I bumped into someone. "Roger! The last person I expected to find here."

"I was looking for you. I thought you might start out with a bit of sightseeing. St. Mark's Square is always the first thing people want to see."

"How did you get here?"

"I came by train yesterday. Let's go to Florians for a coffee. I have some news."

We walked across the square to Florians' impressive entrance.

"This place is incredible, " I said, as we walked in. The ceilings and walls were covered in paintings, mirrors and murals. The whole gave the impression of opulence.

"The cafe was opened in the seventeen hundreds." Roger sounded like a tour guide. "Of course it has been remodelled and extended several times since then. There have of course been many distinguished visitors over the ages. Come on through to the Chinese room. It's my favourite."

"You've been here before?" Paul asked in surprise.

Roger grinned. "No, yesterday was my first time, but you get a feel for things."

We sat on red plush seats at a marble topped table. An attentive waiter took our order.

Roger leant forwards. "I met our contact, and he has given us a lead. There's an art gallery that he thinks is involved in dodgy dealings. I'm following another lead but I would like you to go to the gallery. It's in Calle dei Nova. Have a look around and meet me here at about the same time tomorrow."

"What exactly are we looking for?" Paul asked.

"Anything suspicious." Roger waved his coffee cup. "It might be the headquarters of the gang. Find out who owns it, who manages it. Find out anything you can."

Paul looked at me. "I suppose we could be a couple interested in paintings for our new home?"

"How would we get them back to England?" I asked.

"Good point, but don't try anything elaborate. Just be yourselves, look around and try to chat to whoever is in charge. Both of you are painters. What's more natural than to be interested in other painters and paintings?"

Roger got up. "I must go. See you tomorrow, same place at about three."

"Now we can relax," Paul said, as Roger paid the bill and went back out into the square.

"Let's leave the art gallery for a bit. If you're game we could stroll around, explore. See if we can find a good restaurant for dinner."

We left the crowded square and wandered along the Grand Canal until we reached a side turning on the right-hand side.

"Let's go down here, see where it leads."

The turning led to a narrow alleyway and then through an archway. It was free of tourists, so we walked on until we came out into a small square. On the corner there was a restaurant with tables and chairs outside.

I went up to the board outside displaying the menu. "This looks good, but look at the prices!"

Paul looked at it. "Everything is expensive in Venice, but if you like it we can book for dinner this evening."

I scanned the menu. "It's in Italian. Can you understand it?"

Paul waved his hand. "I don't need to look. I'll go in and book."

I looked admiringly as he confidently disappeared into the interior.

He came out. "All done. It looks good inside. We're booked for eight o'clock."

As we walked across the square, I asked, "Which entrance did we come in by?"

Paul hesitated. "I'm not sure,"

We turned onto a small arched bridge across a canal.

"Well, it wasn't this one." I glanced down at the water as a motorboat made its way slowly under the bridge. We looked at each other and laughed. Retracing our steps we made our way back to St Mark's Square and on to the hotel.

As we picked up our keys at the reception desk, I said, "I don't know about you, but I'm going to settle down with a book until it's time to go out again. Unless you have anything else in mind?"

"I do, but perhaps later. I'll call for you at about seven thirty."

I went to my room and took out my book. It was a thriller, *Time and Time Again*. I read for a while and then sat by the window looking out onto the busy street and the canal.

All these people, I thought, hurrying aimlessly but enjoying themselves. That's what we should be doing. I suddenly realised we hadn't had any lunch. I felt hungry and thirsty. I put my book away and went down to the dining room. I debated whether I should call Paul to see if he would like to join me but decided to go down on my own.

Entering the room, I asked the waiter if it was possible to

have afternoon tea.

"Of course, Signorina, a sandwich, English tea and perhaps some cake?"

"Thank you, that will be fine."

He showed me to a table near the window with a view of the canal.

As I sat waiting I gazed out of the window. Suddenly I caught sight of a familiar face, as a man walked past.

"It's Terry," I said out loud, clutching the table. I got up quickly and went out onto the street, running after the figure I thought was Terry.

I called, "Terry," then as the figure turned I thought for a moment perhaps it was a stranger.

The man stopped and looked back. "Serina, is that you?" It was Terry.

Chapter Twenty-Four

Terry walked back towards me and took me in his arms. "What are you doing here?"

"It's a long story. Look, we can't talk in the street. I was just about to have something to eat. I'm staying in this hotel." I pointed back at the hotel. "Come and join me."

He looked at his watch. "Yes, all right. I've got an appointment in half an hour, but it's great to see you."

I led him back to the hotel and to my table.

The waiter came over. "What would you like, Signor?"

"I've just ordered afternoon tea. Would you like that?" I interrupted.

Terry laughed. "Very English." He spoke in rapid Italian to the waiter who nodded.

"I didn't know you spoke Italian," I said.

"A lot of things have happened since we met at College. I'm married now to a Venetian girl, and I have a job."

"Oh Terry, and you wanted to be a painter. What happened to all those grand ideas you had at college?"

"But I am still a painter. It's an unusual job, but it brings in quite a lot of money. I can't tell you anything else about it as it's hush hush."

Tea arrived and we chatted about our time in college.

"I wonder what happened to Angela?" I asked.

Terry smiled. "I expect she found that rich husband and is now surrounded by a brood of kids. But what about you?"

I gave him a brief account of my life in the Lake District, missing out all the exciting bits and ending up with, "I'm just here on holiday with a friend of mine."

"Aha, a lover."

I felt myself blushing. "Not exactly but you never know."

Terry grinned. "It's a good job I'm married, otherwise . . ."

I thumped his shoulder.

He got up. "Well I must go. How long are you here for?"

"About another week." I mentally crossed my fingers.

"You're staying at this hotel, so I'll give you a ring. Perhaps we can go for a meal, make a foursome and I can meet this lover of yours."

He waved goodbye.

I sat back and reflected on the good times we had at college.

I went back to my room and read until it was time to get ready to go out.

Paul arrived at seven thirty, gave me a hug, and stood admiringly as I slipped a light coat over my simple blue dress.

Making our way back across St Mark's Square, still crowded with tourists, we reached our restaurant, which was also crowded but with what looked like local people.

We were shown to a table at the side.

The restaurant was spacious with three alcoves at the end of the room with tables in them set for a meal.

I looked round the room. "We ought to have booked one of those alcoves."

"I expect they are all booked up. They certainly didn't offer them to me when I booked."

The waitress came up to us, putting a menu in Paul's hand.

"What will you have?" Paul asked, looking at the menu. "I would suggest we start with Sarde in Saor."

"What's that?" I asked.

"Looks like sardines, but it says it's a speciality of the house."

"Let me look." I took the menu and in doing so my gaze fell on a couple in one of the alcoves.

"Don't look now." I covered my face with the menu. "Charles and Isobel are sitting just over there in the corner."

"I don't believe it." Paul swung round to look.

"Turn back," I whispered.

For the rest of the meal I felt uncomfortable, although the food was delicious. We started off with sardines which were served with onions, raisins and pine nuts. Then we went on to Bigoli in Salsa, a delicious pasta, with a glass of a local white wine.

"Would you like a dessert?" Paul asked.

I rubbed my tummy. "No, I don't think so, You have one if you like."

He looked at the menu again but then put it down. "No, let's just finish off with coffee."

"That's fine." I felt as though we were going to be spotted by Charles and Isobel at any moment.

"What should we do? Follow them when they leave?"

"We could try, but I've never tried shadowing someone. I know how they do it in the films but in real life?"

I sat up straight. "They're leaving now, come on. No coffee, we've got to go."

Paul beckoned the waiter. "Can we have our bill please?"

"You don't want coffee, Signor?"

"No, we have to leave."

The bill seemed to take ages coming and by the time Paul paid, Charles and Isobel were gone.

As we stood outside the restaurant there was no sign of them.

"Which way do you think they went?" I asked.

"Search me," Paul grumbled. "We might as well go back our usual way, we might see them."

But we didn't.

"At least we now know that they are here," Paul said, as we reached our hotel.

No lovemaking. We both agreed that we would be good so it was a chaste kiss and we returned to our respective rooms. I just fell into bed and slept well.

Paul called for me the next morning and we went down to breakfast. After breakfast we set off to find the Art Gallery. It was situated in a dingy street just a short walk from the restaurant where we'd dined the previous evening. The gallery looked quite small. It had just one window facing the canal, and there was a narrow entrance.

A solitary painting stood in the window.

"Look at this." Paul drew me over to the window. "Isn't this one of the stolen paintings that they showed us in London?"

I looked carefully at it. "Yes it is."

"I'm going in." Paul pulled open the door. A bell tinkled in the distance.

"Wait for me." I followed him.

When we went in, it was much bigger inside. Brightly lit with pictures adorning the walls, it immediately felt familiar to me.

"It's just like the gallery in Ambleside."

"Can I help you?" a familiar voice said.

I gasped. "Terry, what are you doing here?"

"I work here." He looked across at Paul as though to say *Is this your new boyfriend?*

I caught his look. "Well, yes, I mean no. Paul, this is Terry, a friend from college days."

Paul shook hands a little warily.

"So this was the job you were talking about." I looked round.

"Yes, I run the gallery for Charles . . ."

"Aventine," Paul and I chorused together.

Terry looked surprised. "How did you know?"

We looked at each other.

"You first," Paul said.

"It's a long story, but briefly, Charles Aventine is wanted in England for involvement in stealing and smuggling valuable pictures out of the country. It's obvious now that he brings them here to sell. The one in your window looks like one of the stolen pictures."

Terry laughed. "Well you're wrong there. I painted that one myself some days ago."

"Can we look at it?" Paul asked.

"Of course. I'll take it out of the window for you." Terry opened the back of the window and took the painting out, laying it on the large table at the side of the room by his desk.

Paul examined it closely. "It's a fine piece of work. You say you painted it?"

"Yes, I've got the original downstairs. You say it's stolen?"

"Can we have a look at the original?" I asked.

"Of course, come on down." Terry led us to the back and down a narrow stairway.

"There's no real light down here so it's fitted up with special daylight floodlights, the sort they use in films. Otherwise I couldn't get the colours right."

I looked round the vaulted room, canvases stacked up against the walls.

"Isn't this room under the water?"

"Sure, but it's quite watertight. The Venetian engineers knew a thing or two about tunnelling under water as well as building the canals and buildings."

Over to the side was another painting that Terry was working on.

I turned to Paul. "I've seen this one before. It's one of the stolen ones from the attic."

Terry gripped my hand. "What do you mean and what attic?"

Paul advanced menacingly. "Let go of her."

"Calm down both of you," I said. Is there a coffee shop nearby where we could talk?"

Terry released my hand. "Good idea. There's one just round the corner. Come on, I'll shut up shop. Charles isn't around at the moment."

We went back up into the main gallery. Terry switched off the lights and ushered us out, shutting and locking the door.

Sitting in the small cafe, Terry ordered coffees for us.

"What are you doing making copies of stolen paintings?" Paul asked.

"Charles commissioned me to make copies of some paintings, and also asked me to manage this gallery for him," Terry said. "I don't know anything about stolen paintings, although I've noticed some shady characters visiting when Charles is around. We don't normally get many visitors in an out-of-the-way place like this."

"I can assure you they are stolen paintings. We have a contact here that we can report to," Paul said. "Why don't you come with us and tell him what you've told us?"

"You've got me worried now. I don't want to get mixed up in anything shady. Yes, all right I'll come along but it probably means I'll lose this job."

"Not necessarily, our contact might want you to keep it. Can you meet us at Florians this afternoon at about three o'clock?

"That shouldn't be a problem. See you then."

As we went out I said to Paul, "Terry is obviously innocent, and now we know what Charles and Isobel are up to so we can report it to Roger this afternoon."

We got to Florians a bit before three and found Roger waiting. We were able to give him the whole story before Terry turned up.

Terry was late. "Sorry. A customer came in, so I couldn't

rush."

I introduced him to Roger, who told him the story of the stolen paintings. Then he said, "I would suggest you go back and act as though nothing was wrong. I'll report this to Major Jackson and let him take it from there."

"What about us?" I asked.

"Your work is finished. Go back and enjoy yourself. Meet me here tomorrow just in case, and I will let you know if anything else needs to be done.

Next day when we got there, he told us that Charles and Isobel were living in an apartment above the gallery. The police had raided them and found a stack of stolen paintings in the basement room.

"What about Jed Thompson?" I asked.

"No sign of him," Roger replied. "They probably left him back in the Lake District."

"I don't like the idea of him still running around. He might still be after my house," I said.

Paul put his arm round my waist. "I'm sure your friends at the farm will have kept an eye on your place, so don't worry."

For some reason I seemed determined to worry about something. "What about Terry?" I asked.

"He was arrested, but since he was innocent he will get off," Roger said. "Thanks to both of you for a good job done. I spoke to Major Jackson last night on the phone. He gave me a message for the two of you. Don't hurry back. Spend a couple of days enjoying yourselves as a reward for the good work."

"That's great," Paul said, squeezing my hand. "I think we can manage that, can't we?"

"We certainly can." I was enthusiastic. "I've been looking across the water at that church I can see from my window. I'd like to visit it."

"Good choice," Roger said. "It's the church of Saint Giorgio Maggiore. The facade is magnificent, and inside, the paintings are wonderful. Get around a bit. The Galleria dell' Accademia with its terrific collection of Venetian paintings, the Basilica di San Marco, the Bridge of Sighs, a gondola trip, a couple of days won't be enough, but then you must come back to England."

CHAPTER TWENTY-FIVE

The days went quickly. I saw the marvellous paintings in the church across the water. The academic gallery of paintings astounded me.

"I'll never be able to paint like that," I said to Paul as I looked at one of the paintings.

"Every painter has their own individual style. I've seen your paintings, and they are good."

On our last day we took a gondola ride.

"Our last day." I sighed as we sat in the richly decorated gondola, painted with shiny black varnish.

The gondolier pointed to the six-pronged device on the boat's prow. "It is a symbol that was used on Roman ships," he said proudly.

Obviously a man who enjoyed his work and kept his gondola in top condition.

Relaxing on cushions, we watched as he took us along the Grand Canal to the Bridge of Sighs. We passed other gondolas gliding gently through the water. A vaporetto, water taxi, chugged slowly past.

"This is the life." I stretched out lazily.

Our gondolier poled us expertly to the landing stage.

Paul helped me out and paid the gondolier, who waved his broad brimmed hat and was gone.

Back at the hotel we decided to have dinner there and then pack ready for departure.

I phoned Sonia at the farm to let her know I would be back the next day. "It will probably be late when we get there."

"That's no problem. I'll get Nancy to air the bed for you and get some food in."

"We'll have a meal somewhere on the way back, so don't worry."

"At least I'll get something in for your breakfast."

Next day the trip home was uneventful. Motorboat back to Marco Polo airport, plane back to City Airport and train to Windermere. We ate a meal in the dining car on the way as it would be late when we arrived home.

We phoned ahead and were met at Windermere station by Sid Chapman, who drove us to my cottage.

"Do you want me to come in and check the place out?" Paul asked hopefully.

I opened the door and switched on the main light. Paul followed me in carrying my suitcase. He closed the door behind him. Immediately I was in his arms and our lips met in a passionate kiss.

"I've been wanting to do that all day," Paul said, holding me close. "But you must be exhausted after all that travelling."

"So must you. I don't think I want to do much except flop into bed. I'm not even going to unpack. Come over in the morning."

"Fine, I'll come over at eight, assuming I can get the old car going."

"Make it a bit later and then you can have breakfast with me. Nancy will have brought us some food."

He gave me another kiss and a hug, then went back out to where Sid was waiting for him.

Now that Paul was gone, the house felt lonely. Putting on all the lights, I realised how deeply I was involved with Paul. I made myself a hot drink and went to bed.

It seemed only moments after there was a heavy knocking at the front door.

Sleepily I slipped on a dressing gown and went down stairs. When I opened the door Jed Thompson almost fell into the room.

He still looked and smelt as he always did but there was a look of desperation on his face.

"Can you help me?" He staggered, clutching at my arm.

I stepped back in alarm.

"How did you know I was back, and why should I help you? You stole my paintings and goodness knows what else you are into."

"The police are after me. I don't know which way to turn. You're my only hope."

He looked so desperate that I forgot for a moment how devious he could be.

"How can I possibly help you?" I asked.

"I need food and a car. My Land Rover is too well-known. If you come up to the waterfall above Windemere in your car with just some bread, cheese and some water and let me borrow your car, I can get away. I'll abandon the car somewhere without harming it so you will get it back. You can take the Land Rover."

I thought desperately for a moment. If I contacted Paul and the police, perhaps we could trap him.

"All right," I said. "Give me an hour and I'll be there."

Jed muttered a gruff *thanks* and was off.

I quickly dressed in sweater and slacks, packed some bread, cheese and a bottle of water in a plastic carrier bag, then put a coat over my shoulders.

I rang Paul and told him what was happening.

"Hold on until I get there," he said. "I'll alert the police and we should be able to catch him red handed."

I looked at my watch. Almost an hour had gone by. I

couldn't afford to wait for Paul or the police. Perhaps I could stall Jed until they arrived. Paul would surely guess I was at the waterfall. I packed the food, water and a torch into the car and started off.

It was a moonlit night. The trees threw eerie shadows on the road ahead of me. I pulled into the deserted car park. Not quite deserted, Jed's Land Rover was already there. As I stopped, a torch flashed from the direction of the falls. I took the key out of the ignition and headed off, stumbling over the rough ground clutching my torch. To my surprise, the flash was coming not from the base of the falls—its beam came somewhere near the top. I realised that it was coming from the bridge above the falls, so using my torch I made my way up the track to the bridge. Halfway across I could see a dark figure. I shone the torch and there was an answering flash. Knowing how decrepit the bridge was, I went across it holding tight to the handrail, meeting Jed in the middle. When I reached him, he grabbed me in a firm grip. The smell of him was overpowering.

The bridge swayed as I struggled in his arms. The roar of the waterfall filled my ears.

"Got you at last, my beauty. You're the one who has been causing me all this trouble." He forced me up against the handrail.

"Don't be a fool, Jed," I gasped. "You can't get away with it."

"Oh, can't I?" He lifted me up. "It's a long way down and I don't think you will survive."

As he spoke his foot slipped and instead of throwing me over the falls, he slid under the rail, letting go of me and crashing down into the frothing water below.

I grabbed the rail. My arms felt as though they were being wrenched out of their sockets as I managed to haul myself back on to the bridge just as Paul flung himself onto the rickety structure and held me in his arms.

"I'm sorry I took so long." He caressed me. "The car wouldn't start at first until I persuaded it. Why didn't you wait for me at the cottage?"

"I thought I was doing the right thing." I nestled into his arms.

"You're trembling like a leaf." He held me close.

"Leaves don't tremble unless they have a reason."

I felt good in his arms, relaxing after my ordeal. Our lips met and I gave myself up to him in a long languorous kiss.

"Not quite the right time, but will you marry me?"

Lights flashed on the ground below.

"What a time to ask," I said breathlessly, looking down. "At least the police seem to have arrived. Let's get off this bridge."

"Is that a *yes?*" he asked.

"It's maybe for now. I need to recover my wits." I pushed him gently along the swaying construction.

When we reached the base of the falls, two policemen were pulling Jed out of the water.

"He'll live." Sergeant Hastings scratched his head. "He was lucky not to have cracked his skull on a rock, but we've got him now and he will talk. He's that sort."

Paul put his arm round me and I drew close to him.

"Don't you worry, Miss. Just go home with your young man and let us deal with this." Sergeant Hastings smiled at us.

"Come on, my young man." I gave Paul a push.

He looked down at me. "Okay, your place or mine?"

"Mine, of course. I'll follow you in my car."

CHAPTER TWENTY-SIX

Next day with my thoughts on churches I remembered that I had promised Roger Flatley to find out where Aunt Em was buried. I assumed he would be back, so I rang him up.

"You're back. Does that mean everything is finished now?"

"Not quite," he said. "One or two loose ends, but mostly done. What can I do for you?"

"I suddenly remembered that I would find out about Aunt Em's grave for you."

"Don't worry. I've been rather busy now that Charles Aventine and Isobel Santir have both been caught. Incidentally, I got my paintings back. They were among the ones found in Venice. "

"That's good. I expect you have heard about my experience with Jed Thompson?"

"I've heard more than that. When's the wedding?"

I blushed. "Soon. I don't have any parents left, so Paul's parents are arranging it for us."

"Don't forget to invite me. Now, what about Emily's grave?"

"She's buried in St. Mary's church in Ambleside. Would you like me to come with you to see the grave?"

"Yes, I would. When can we go?"

"How about tomorrow? Paul and I are going to St. Mary's church to meet the vicar."

We all went together in Paul's car. The Vicar was there to greet us and took Paul into the vestry of the church.

Roger and I went into the graveyard to where Aunt Em was buried. A simple gravestone marked the spot. Roger knelt by the graveside, placing a small posy of flowers on the grave.

I stayed discreetly in the background.

As he stood at the graveside I could hear him speaking softly.

"I'm sorry I didn't come back sooner while you were still alive," he said. "I thought of you every day and I know you got my letters but then I was sent on a mission that landed me behind enemy lines. I got knocked out by the blast from a shell and left for dead. That was why there were no more letters. I was rescued from death but lost my memory. I had a compulsion to come back here but I didn't know why. Now I do." He broke down and cried, tears streaming down his cheeks.

When he looked up I stretched out my hand to him without speaking.

Paul came back from the church and we proceeded in silence, through the lych-gate and into the car.

We dropped Roger at his cottage. I wanted to stay with him, but he assured us that he was all right.

Paul's parents had been delighted to hear that Paul and I were to be married and immediately offered to arrange the wedding reception.

On the day of the wedding, the church was packed with local painters, and after the ceremony, as Paul and I left the church, we found ourselves under an archway of paint brushes wielded by all our friends. The reception was held at Paul's home with a disco to follow.

Paul and I circulated and danced a little in the disco, which was held in the large conservatory adjoining the house.

"It's as good as a tent," Artero said. "It's where I do some of my painting, but we cleared it all out for the dancing, if you can call it that dancing." He looked disapprovingly at the gyrating bodies.

Secretly I agreed with him. Proper ballroom dancing was what I loved, and I was pleased when Paul spoke to Rob, the DJ, who then played an old-fashioned waltz just for us.

Eventually we felt able to leave our guests. Lucinda had set aside a room for us to change into ordinary clothes. When we made our way downstairs, everyone gathered to see us on our way. Paul's car was decorated with streamers, a big notice on the back *Just Married* with tin cans tied on behind with lengths of string. We went out quickly, ducking the confetti thrown at us. Paul started the car and drove off leaving behind a cheering, laughing crowd.

Paul was very mysterious about what was to happen next.

I had asked him several times what arrangements we should make for the honeymoon.

He just said, "Leave it to me."

"Where are we going?" I insisted as we left.

"Wait until we stop and get this paraphernalia off the car and then I will tell you."

He turned into a lay-by just off the main road.

I helped him remove the streamers, the notice and the cans, depositing them in the roadside bin.

"So where are we going?" I asked again.

He took two tickets out of his pocket. "I hope you don't mind going to Venice again. It was Artero's idea. A chance to see all those beautiful paintings, visit the churches and museums we didn't manage to do on the last trip."

"It's a great idea." I snuggled up to him. "A trip in a gondola as well?"

"Of course, but first we have to get to Manchester Airport. Our bags are packed, and I've booked us into the Airport Hotel for tonight. We fly tomorrow morning."

We took the morning flight to Venice, and after a water taxi ride to the main island, we settled into a luxurious hotel on the Grand Canal. Not the same one as before, but equally nice.

"All painters should come to Venice," I said as we dined that evening in the small restaurant round the corner from the Grand Canal where we'd dined before, and next day we began a tour of the churches, seeing many famous paintings, and of course we had a trip in a gondola.

I sank back on the silken cushions of the gondola. Paul was mine forever, and we would face whatever life could throw at us together.

The End

About the Author

Pippa Newnton first began writing stories at school. Encouraged by her English teacher, she submitted them to magazines only to have them rejected. She kept writing and was eventually published in her university magazine. Since then she has had short stories published in a variety of women's magazines. Her first novel, *Whispers in the Mind'*, was published by Extasy Books.

This book *Love in the Lakes* was written because of her love of the English Lake District.

www.ingramcontent.com/pod-product-compliance
Lightning Source LLC
LaVergne TN
LVHW010106170826
845678LV00012B/2263

* 9 7 8 1 4 8 7 4 3 8 1 0 4 *